THE PATREON COLLECTION

VOLUME 5

STEFON MEARS

Also by Stefon Mears

Cavan Oltblood Series
Half a Wizard
The Ice Dagger
Spells of Undeath

Spells for Hire
Devil's Shoestring
Zombie Powder
Spirit Trap
Dragon's Blood

The Rise of Magic
Magician's Choice
Sleight of Mind
Lunar Alchemy
Three Fae Monte
The Sphinx Principle
Double Backed Magic (coming soon)

The Telepath Trilogy
Surviving Telepathy
Immoral Telepathy
Targeting Telepathy

Edge of Humanity
Caught Between Monsters
Hunting Monsters

Power City Tales
Not Quite Bulletproof
No Money in Heroism

Sects and the City (coming soon)
Prince of a Thousand Worlds (coming soon)
Longhairs and Short Tales: A Collection of Cat Stories
Devil's Night
Portal-Land, Oregon
Stealing from Pirates
Fade to Gold
With a Broken Sword
Twice Against the Dragon
The House on Cedar Street
Sudden Death
On the Edge of Faerie
Confronting Legends (Spells & Swords Vol. 1)
Uncle Stone Teeth and Other Macabre Poems
The Patreon Collection, Vol. 1-5 (Vol. 6, coming soon)

ISBN: 978-1-948490-18-4

THE PATREON COLLECTION

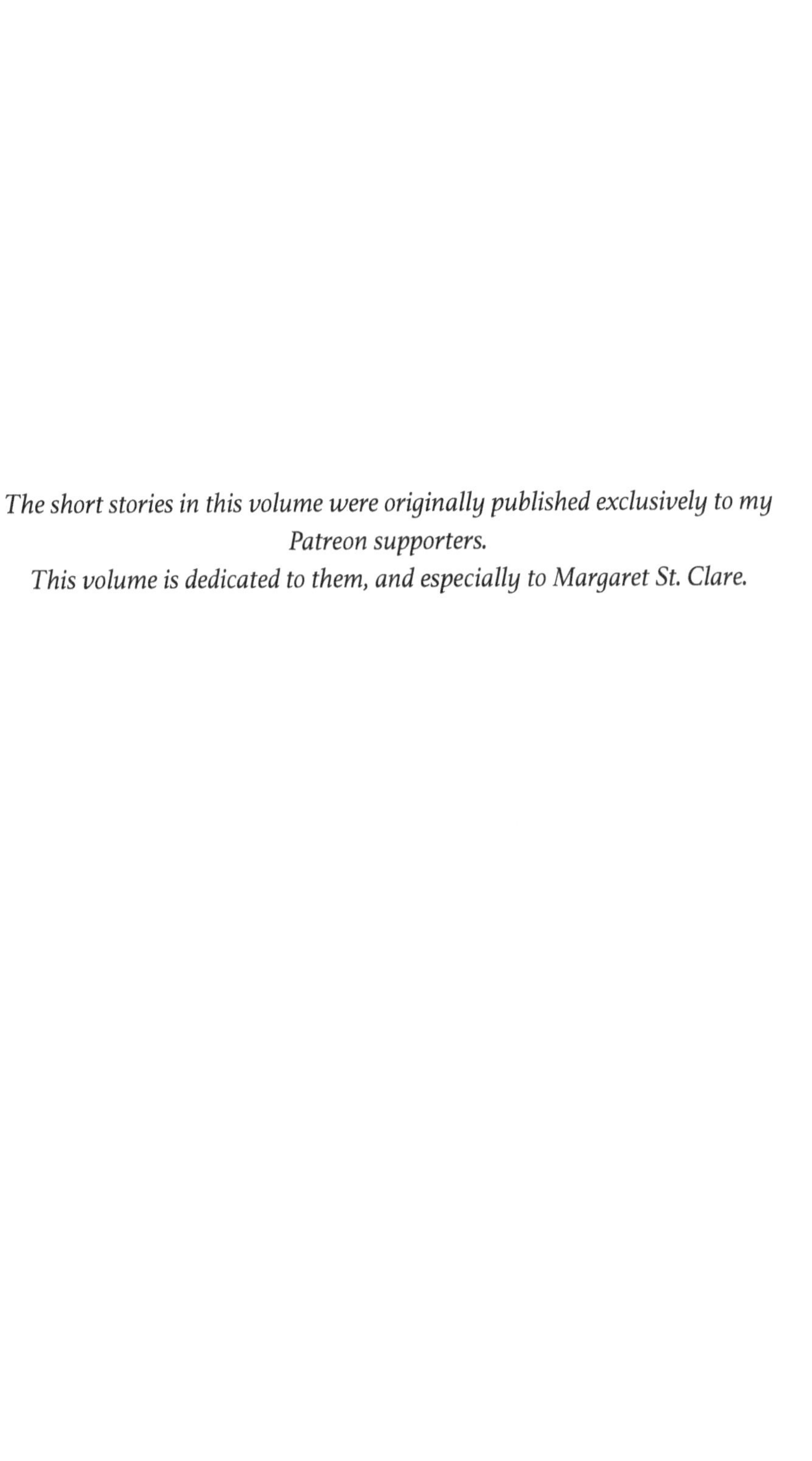

The short stories in this volume were originally published exclusively to my Patreon supporters.
This volume is dedicated to them, and especially to Margaret St. Clare.

CONTENTS

FOREWORD

As I write this introduction, pretty much the whole world is coping with COVID-19. And a major, worldwide event like this is a weird time to be a writer.

See, there's a part of me that wants to hide and watch the news. Or get updates from my wife, the registered nurse. But I bring myself to my desk every day, and the power of habit helps me keep writing through the chaos. Writing becomes my escape from the madness happening outside my door.

I escape into stories. And I know I'm not alone in this.

That's the other weird thing about being a writer at a time like this. On the one hand, what I do isn't important. I'm not out there saving lives, like doctors, nurses, and other medical professionals. I'm not keeping people in food and essentials, the way restaurants, grocery stores and the like are doing. And there are others out there, doing the jobs that keep our countries and cities running, and keep us able to continue living in at least a semblance of the way we're accustomed to.

Me, on the other hand. I'm just sitting at my desk telling stories. No one lives or dies on what I do.

Still, I think storytelling has a kind of second or third-tier level of importance. Because everyone needs a break from the news and the worries.

If that's you, I hope these stories give you the escape you're looking for.

Inside this volume you'll find a decent array of options, mostly fantasy. Dark fantasy ("Running for Health"), historical fantasy ("The Forgotten Rebel"), traditional fantasy ("Shadow of a Curse"), mythic fantasy ("The Trials of Rebirth"), detective fantasy ("Staring Down the Barrel of a Wand") and more.

All kinds of moods, and all kinds of stories, twelve in all. And all of them, of course, first published to my Patreon readers between January and June of 2019.

Happy reading,
Stefon

RUNNING FOR HEALTH

I sometimes will start a story with no idea where it's going. I'll just pick something I actually do from time to time, put a character who is *not* me in that situation, and see what my mind comes up with.

I wonder what it says about me that more of those stories turn out to be horror or dark fantasy than happy and uplifting fantasy tales.

Anyway, this is one such tale. There's a middle school in my neighborhood, with a track very much like the one I describe here. And I've been out running on that track after twilight, very much like the guy in this story.

Of course, by the time I wrote this story, I was doing most of my running on a treadmill in my basement.

Coincidence? I'm not so sure...

It was the first and last time I tried running at dusk.

Running was still a new idea to me then. As exercise, I mean. I'd been sitting on my ass for long enough that my couch was developing a distinct dent in my favorite spot, and I couldn't keep pretending that my jeans were just shrinking in the wash.

No. The fact was that ever since I'd moved to Portland, Oregon, I'd let myself get sedentary.

It was easy enough to do. My old basketball friends were still back in the Bay Area, and I didn't know the courts around here. Not that there were all that many courts in the west hills of Portland.

Plus, I don't know if you knew this, but it rains in Portland. No, I don't mean it sprinkles a little bit now and again. I mean it *rains*. My first month in town I saw more rain than I might have seen back in Santa Clara in two years. Didn't come down in buckets. It came down in hot tubs. In swimming pools. All winter long, when it wasn't making a token effort at snowing, it rained.

And when it wasn't raining, it was chilly and overcast, even in April, when I first poked my head out and considered trying to get back into shape. All that rain and chill made it easy for me to say, "I'll find a court later," then turn on some re-run or other and spend the evening in more or less the same spot on the couch.

Must have been six or seven months I'd been doing this. Snacking. Loafing, and generally doing the kinds of nothing that would make it harder to find a girlfriend here in my new city.

I needed to get out of the apartment more. And not just for my health. For my sanity. I worked from home – telecommuting to the three different places I did technical writing for – so on the days I didn't got out, I didn't see another living soul.

So on the dating side, it wasn't as though I was going to meet a girl at work. Plus, how many girls would want to meet my expanding waistline? Well, I didn't know, but I suspected the answer wasn't one I'd like.

So, I took up running.

I lived on a hill, so I didn't start trying to run the streets of my neighborhood, but there was a high school just at the end of the block, so I would drive my car down there, park, and run on their track.

Yes, I drove a block so I could exercise. Seemed like the smart move at the time, and truth to tell, it paid off that day.

Anyway, I began by running at lunchtime, because it was June and school was out. But when two of the places that gave me contract work started needing me to hit tighter deadlines around the middle of the month, my chances to run started bleeding later and later into the afternoon. Once in a while, they even led to me running on that tarmac track under the sodium lights.

See, the track surrounded the football field, and this school must have had a heck of a team. They kept that grass watered and mown and game-ready year-round, and surrounding it they had the kind of grandstands that I expected to see at college stadiums.

I had to enter and leave the track by coming down what felt like a tunnel, even though it was open to the sky above. It was just the height of the grandstands that made it seem like a tunnel.

I admit, when I first showed up to start running there, I was kind of jealous. My high school had been a rinky-dink public place that barely managed a set of bleachers on each side of the field. And our gym was so decrepit that I would have sworn its concrete was ready to come down around us every time I set foot on the old, worn basketball court.

But this fancy high school here in Portland. If I'd gone here, I might have taken my basketball more seriously. Might have gotten recruited for college. Maybe even gotten to the NBA.

Well, maybe not. I was tall, but closer to six feet than seven, and I never could shoot with my left hand. Still, those were the sorts of pleasant thoughts I allowed myself that day as the sun began to set. I was decked out in my running shorts and athletic shoes – special running shoes, because if I was going to do this, I was going to do it right – and a mesh tee shirt that was supposed to whisk away sweat. Even had my long brown hair tied back in a ponytail.

I'd stretched on the asphalt of the parking lot, daydreaming about the NBA, and wondered why my car was the only one here. It had been a nice day. Not too hot, not too cold, even with evening coming on. The smell of fresh-mown grass coming from the field.

All right, coming from the stadium.

And I had the place to myself. Weird, but not so weird that it stopped me from trotting down the almost-tunnel toward the track.

The lights weren't on up above, not yet, and with the grandstands around me, the dark seemed to rise faster on the track than it had in the parking lot.

But my eyes had no trouble adjusting. I'd run at night before, and I didn't imagine running at dusk would be all that much different.

More the fool I was.

⁂

I WAS JUST STARTING TO GET LOOSE, TROTTING MY WARM-UP PACE ON the first lap around the tarmac. Pretending that the grandstands around me were full of adoring fans, cheering me on to setting some kind of world record for distance running.

The air got a little chillier on my skin, the first hints of sweat starting. Not effort sweat, not yet, just that light acknowledgment that my body was moving, and not sure how it felt about this.

My legs felt good about it. Even through just the light warm-up, I had that good feeling starting in my thighs and calves. Blood pumping. Muscles getting ready. If I were playing basketball, they would be telling me that the time for warm-up was over, and I needed to get a game going, or at least run some layups. Something like that.

But I wasn't playing basketball, and I wasn't quite sure yet how running worked, for the long haul. I knew my legs were ready, but I wasn't sure yet about my back and my knees. Different sort of exercise, running. Constant movement, instead of the starting and stopping of basketball. I wanted to make sure my whole body was ready before I picked up the pace.

I was just about ready to make that shift, when I heard something strange.

Now, I knew the sounds of running pretty well. My shoes on the tarmac, beating out a slow but steady pace. The distant whistle of the wind, and the even more distant honking of the occasional car horn, or the rapid whine of a motorcycle.

With no other runners around me, those were the sounds I expected. The sounds I'd been hearing in the ten minutes or so I'd been out here.

But now I was hearing something else too.

Another set of shoes, running.

It was only one other set. It shouldn't have been anything to draw my attention. Except that I knew I'd been alone out here, and welcomed the company. It might even have been a girl. Someone I could run with, get back in shape with.

All right, I was lonely. New town, and spending all my time at home.

Anyway, I glanced around to see who my new running partner was.

But there was no one.

I got this creeping sensation up my back then, and a flutter in my stomach that had nothing to do with the turkey-and-swiss sandwich waiting for me in my refrigerator at home.

I could hear that second set of running shoes. Echoing my every step, but not a literal echo.

This place did have a bit of an echo. The grandstands were only too happy to bounce sound back to me. But my shoes, well, they didn't make enough sound for an echo. Especially not an echo that sounded like it was coming from behind me.

Not right behind me. Not yet. But maybe a quarter of the way back down the track.

And keeping pace.

"Hello?" I called out, hoping that I was hearing things. That maybe the rising dusk and the stadium were playing games with my imagination. That there was someone there, and I just hadn't seen them in my glances back.

No one answered me though.

That creeping sensation went straight up my neck then, and my shoulders shivered as though someone was breathing down my neck.

I picked up my pace.

So did my echo.

And the worst part about that? The part that made some of the muscles low in my torso seize up?

There was a slight delay before the echo sped up.

I wasn't alone out here.

———

I TRIED TO REASSURE MYSELF. I WAS BEING SILLY. SURE, THE DARK WAS rising here in the stadium, but it wasn't full night yet. I couldn't really see more than a star or two up above, and the sodium lights above the field had yet to blaze into incandescence.

So it had to be nerves. Nerves and isolation, playing games with my ears.

I told myself that over and over until I started believing it. Believing that there'd been no delay before my echo sped pace to match me. That the echo was just my own shoes, the sound reflecting from someplace I'd never noticed when there were other runners around. That it didn't sound like there was someone running no more than fifty yards behind me.

I kept telling myself those things.

Until the echo sped up.

Ice all through my veins then, and an extra layer of cold sweat poured out over the good exercise sweat I'd started building.

Wasn't much of a change, speed-wise. It wasn't from a trot to a sprint. But it was a faster trot, and that scared the hell out of me. Got my heart going more than the running would.

And I found myself speeding up too.

I matched the echo, and then I pushed a little faster.

The echo waited a full five seconds before matching my pace.

Whatever it was behind me, it was playing with me now. It knew I knew it was there.

And it started going just a little bit faster.

I could have kicked myself then. I'd just passed the exit. I wanted to get the hell out of here, but there were only a handful of ways to do that. Most of them required me to go up into the stands, find their exit tunnels, and hope the doors at the other end were open.

Yeah, that didn't sound like a great option to me.

The only other choice was to leave by the field exit. Down the almost-tunnel, that was getting farther and farther away with each step, and would only get father still until I came around the curve.

And the thing behind me – the thing I still couldn't see when I looked back over my shoulder – it kept its pace just a tiny bit ahead of my own. Matching, then accelerating just a hair. Until I matched and accelerated again.

In theory, I could keep this going until I got back to the exit.

It practice, it had to know I wanted to do that.

And I couldn't trust that this thing was only just trying to get back into shape, the way I was. It might have been capable of much, much more.

I glanced back as I got to the center of the short end of the oblong. I was now as far from the exit as I could be, but soon there would be angles I could cut across without having to run past ... whatever it was.

And that glance was the first time I saw my pursuer.

Well, I didn't get a good look. Not that time. What I saw was just a shimmer in the air. A distortion that extended maybe six feet above the tarmac. Maybe a little more, but not much.

It was enough. Visual confirmation of what I'd been hearing.

There *was* something behind me. Closing the gap.

That redoubled the chills going down my spine. Pushed my pace faster.

The thing matched me again, and my body reminded me just how new I was to all this. With my heart going double-time from the stress and the effort, and my guts trying to cramp up against the unknown, and now my bladder telling me that it could quite happily express itself if I gave it the chance. With all these things going on, my breaths came faster and shorter, and I swear I already began to tire.

Now, I'd only been at this running thing for a few weeks. But I'd played basketball for many years. I knew my body pretty well. I knew how much it took to tire my body out, and what kind of effort I should have been able to expect from it.

And my body, it shouldn't have been that tired. Not yet. Not even with the extra stress and the increased speed. My body was definitely more tired than it should have been.

And when I glanced back, again, the shimmer looked more pronounced.

I could see an outline now. And this outline looked all too much like what I saw in the mirror every morning.

Panic hit me harder than the elbow of an overactive rebounder.

I cut straight across the grass. I gave up all pretense of exercise and kicked straight up to a sprint.

The only problem was that I'd only gotten maybe a third the way down the track when I did this. Even cutting across the grass, I had a good hundred yards to cover before I reached the almost-tunnel, and that didn't count how many more steps I had to go to get to my car.

But I had to get away from here. From ... it.

It made a sound then. The first sound I'd heard from it, apart from the shoes. Sounded like a wail, but just as much like the sound of a rusty fender bending way too far.

I got maybe ten steps before I realized it wasn't breathing down my neck.

In fact, it sounded farther behind me. Like maybe it had to run to the point I'd reached before it could cut across the grass.

I hoped I was right and poured on the speed. Pushing like this was a fast break for game point. One layup between me and victory.

The turf under my shoes was smooth and level, the grass cushioning every step. Wet though, maybe from afternoon watering. I recognized that in the back of my mind, but the front of my mind was fixed on the goal.

I could see the almost-tunnel ahead of me. Fifty yards, maybe. And beyond it, lights. As though the rest of the world had decided night had risen and turned on their porch lights and street lights, even though the stadium still glowered in gloom.

I had company on the grass then. I could hear it behind me, padding through the grass as fast as I was. And I was pushing my poor legs for all they could do.

But then the thing pushed even faster.

I had to match it. I had enough of a lead – at least, I hoped I did – but not if it started gaining on me.

I don't know why, but I was sure it couldn't leave the stadium. That if I made it out the tunnel, I'd be back in the nice, safe, normal world I knew and out of this death race against something like my own reflection.

So I pushed harder. My legs burned with effort. My lungs too. My side cramped up. My whole body begged me to just drop onto this nice, cushy grass and rest. My body even tried to promise that the whole thing would turn out to be a mistake. A misunderstanding. That it was just another runner, using me as a pacer. Somebody who just happened to look a little like me, from a distance, in the low light.

And I wanted to believe this.

I wanted to believe it enough that I stole a glance over my shoulder.

And I saw me bearing down on me. No more than two dozen steps behind me now, and pushing faster.

And that expression. I don't know that I've ever felt as much hate as I saw in that weird reflection of myself.

Terrified me though. Enough that my body quit arguing. Well, apart from my bladder, which gave up and let loose.

Apart from that, everything I had was going into reaching that almost-tunnel.

And I did. I got to that almost-tunnel, my shoes pounding across the tarmac once more, my lungs ready to burst now, and the world starting to develop a red haze.

But I could hear the thing behind me. I could hear its shoes beating the tarmac too.

And it was gaining. Maybe a dozen paces behind me now.

I screamed and threw everything I had into fleeing. Every primal instinct I possessed. Every ounce of my will to live. Everything that made me who I was, and not just what that thing behind me was trying to become.

I made it to my car.

I ripped open the door of my red Honda Accord and damn near slammed it on my foot, getting it closed behind me.

I looked back at my pursuer. The thing that looked more and more like me with every step.

But the moment that door closed, it vanished. Mid-step. Not even the ripple left in the air to mark its presence.

I locked the door anyway. And I lay my head on the steering wheel. Just panting and wheezing and clutching my cramp and trying to swallow. Sweat burned my eyes. I couldn't hear anything except my own heartbeat, beating so hard and fast I swear it skipped beats once in a while, just for a little rest of its own.

When my breaths were only shaky, I looked up. Glanced around the parking lot.

Still empty. Still no one here but me. And no sign of that ripple. That doppelganger. Whatever it was.

Not until I looked in the mirror, anyway.

When I glanced at myself in my car's rear view mirror, my reflection was just a beat behind me. Just a hair. Little enough that I might not have noticed it. Not if I hadn't just been all too aware of something that looked like me, something that followed me not quite in sync with my movements.

I had to swallow twice, before I could speak. When I managed, I croaked out, "You're gone, right?"

My reflection didn't answer. Didn't betray any signs at all.

Except that when I looked away and looked back, it was just a fraction of a second slower.

And maybe, just maybe, I was seeing a hint of smile in its eyes.

By the time full dark rose, my reflection wasn't playing games anymore. It mirrored me perfectly again. And I felt steady enough to start my car and head for home.

Over the next few days, I kept a sharp eye on my reflection. It seemed to be behaving itself.

Within a week, that started feeling silly. And I started believing it had all been just a trick of the light. That there'd never been anything after me. That the loneliness and the isolation had just started getting to me.

Deep down, though, I knew the truth. There had been something chasing me that day. Something that almost caught me. Something that vanished only when the air between us was cut off by a closing car door.

I might not have admitted the truth. But I knew it.

And I only went running in the daylight, after that.

THE NIGHT OF ABSINTHE
AND REGRET

One question writers get a lot is whether or not people from their own lives show up in their stories. The short answer is no. At least for me. But the longer answer is a little more complicated.

See, I'm pretty sure that aspects of people I know show up in aspects of characters I create. And in this story, that happens in a sideways kind of method. Even for me.

Back in my late teens and early twenties, I performed with several Rocky Horror casts. I developed a number of casual acquaintances, including one without whom this story couldn't have been written.

He does not appear in this story. Not in any way, shape or form.

But his old *apartment* absolutely does. He rented a studio apartment in an old Victorian house that had been segmented into separate apartments. I used the rough layout of that building and back yard – though not the acquaintance's apartment itself – as the setting for this story.

Never thought I'd be breaking into my own apartment, but I couldn't carry any metal with me. So no keys.

Not a problem, though. I knew which window in the back bedroom didn't quite close all the way. Caused a lot of problems keeping the bedroom warm in the winter, the way the cold air would just seep through it. Right now, though, I was grateful.

The apartment building was a converted Victorian house. Four of us had our own rooms there, and we shared a communal kitchen. I was lucky enough to have gotten the master suite, so I had my own sitting room, bathroom, walk-in closet, and enough space for my own refrigerator.

Pretty sweet setup, for the price. Even if the landlord never upgraded anything he didn't have to.

Cheap bastard never spent a dime more than the law required.

It was a warm July night, just the way I remembered it. And I remembered every detail about that night. Not just because it was – had been – only last week, but for the reason I'd been willing to volunteer to test the tachyon temporal displacer.

This was the night that Julie dumped me.

Muggy, July air. Muggy wasn't common in this little Bay Area suburb of Thousand Pines. But for some reason, we'd been having unseasonal rain this year, only not tonight. Not the night I went back to, that is. That night it just threatened all night, air so thick with want of rain that it stuck my semi-cotton jumpsuit to my body.

Whatever this material was, they just had to make it silver. Like this was some Fifties SF movie. They, being the boys upstairs who funded my little department. I think they liked the idea of time travel a little too much. Every email and text message they'd sent for the past week — or would send in the coming week, I should say – had been chock full of time travel jokes.

If I saw one more warning about attempts on Hitler's life...

Anyway, just being in the past, even only a week in the past, gave me this weird sense of déjà vu. Like an echo reverberating nonstop, all through my body. A little distracting, but nothing I couldn't handle.

After all, I was a man on a mission. And I only had another ten minutes to accomplish it.

And so I paid strict attention to all my sensory details, to try to hold myself in my current present. I could hear crickets and frogs, way more than I would have heard most summers, but just the way I remembered from that – from this, I mean – night. All that rain must have been good for them.

I could smell the fresh mown grass from next door, past the redwood privacy fence. The grass *I* stood on was greening up from all the rain, but it was still mostly crabgrass and weeds from my land-lord's neglect.

Then again, that's why my back bedroom window still didn't shut right. I'd stopped complaining after the third time he'd ignored me.

The weird thing, apart from that echoey sensation I mean, was that I could taste two things at once. I could taste the last dregs of my good Puerto Rican coffee, the last cup of which I'd had no more than twenty minutes ago, by my body clock. A good fifteen minutes before they strapped me in and started the machine.

But I could also taste garlic bread, and that was wrong.

That was wrong because the me that belonged in this time actu-ally was tasting garlic bread. It was seven-oh-three p.m., and Julie and I were at that little Italian place downtown. They'd just brought us a basket of garlic bread while we looked over the menu.

I shouldn't have been able to taste that garlic bread, not current me. I hadn't had any garlic bread in a week. Had to have been some resonance effect related to that echo sensation.

I made a mental note about it, then wiped some sweat from my forehead. This semi-cotton jumpsuit didn't breathe right for this kind of weather.

I had about nine minutes of real time before I got yanked back to the present. Way more than I—

What was that?

I could hear something from inside the apartment building. Wait. It was a Thursday. Wasn't that the night that Simone from upstairs did yoga in the backyard?

Crap. I'd forgotten.

I couldn't let her see me. I mean, even apart from this outfit, she knew I was out with Julie. Couldn't leave evidence that I'd been here.

I hustled over to the window, whipped it open, and scrambled inside to fall onto my old, creaky king-size bed.

The size was the only really good thing about that bed. It was old enough now that the springs bitched every time I rolled over on it. Had to admit though, it did make ... other activities ... sound more impressive.

I got the window closed before Simone rounded the corner. She looked great as always, a willowy redhead dressed in clingy, stretchy basic black and carrying her yoga mat. Simone could have modeled for yoga calendars. She had that kind of body and that kind of smile.

In fact, it was that smile – and let's be honest, that body – that had caused my trouble in the first place.

No time for that now.

I rolled off of the bed onto the floor, and realized I was still hearing a noise from inside the house. On this floor.

At my front door.

No. That couldn't be. I knew for a fact that Julie and I were still at the restaurant. I could taste the Italian coffee we'd ordered, and I could still taste that strong garlic bread.

So who was trying to open my front door?

I crossed the squeaky wood in two dozen quick paces, stepping over and around the piles of books and magazines I went through like a fiend, yet never managed to find room for on my many book-shelves.

Probably because I needed more bookshelves, but I was out of wall space.

I got to my front door, and picked up my baseball bat from the umbrella stand...

And immediately dropped it.

I couldn't hit someone who came in. Could I? I mean, they had to have actually come in last time, didn't they?

Or, wait, the last time was this time, wasn't it? I mean, this is a week ago, which means that last week, while I was at the restaurant with Julie, I was actually here, wasn't I?

Wait, if that were true, then this whole mission was doomed to failure.

I dove to the other side of my oversized, overstuffed brown couch and hid. I needed time to figure this out, and I didn't have it. I was down under eight minutes now, and someone was working the knob of my door like they had a key or could pick the lock.

I needed to think.

Last week – I mean tonight – Julie had come home with me after our date. Nothing special in and of itself, except that any night with Julie was special. No, the problem didn't come until later that night. When Julie had gone to the bathroom, and found Simone's panties down on the floor, behind my garbage can.

If I'd only remembered to take my garbage out a few days ago, I could have thrown them out with the garbage, and Julie would never have known about my drunken dalliance with Simone. She'd never have dumped me.

It was all so stupid. Simone wasn't into me. I wasn't into her. But she had that bottle of absinthe, and we'd both always wanted to try it. And a drink became four, and then we were laughing at every little thing, and then she started showing me yoga poses, and then...

Well, her panties did end up on my bathroom floor. Strange that she didn't think to find them.

Come to think of it, if I'd traveled a few days further, I could have just taken out the garbage, and...

No. The warning signs were all there in the math that I'd gone over with the team at least a dozen times while prepping for this trip. No more than a week exactly into the past. Which meant tonight. Which meant while Julie and I were at the restaurant. No leaving evidence that I'd been there, which meant I couldn't have taken out the garbage, even if I did at least grab those panties.

Whoever was at the knob started knocking.

I blinked in confusion then. If they had the key, why would they...

I smacked myself in the forehead. Someone had the wrong room.

I moved up to the door and, gruffing my voice down a half an octave, said, "What?"

"I'm looking for Andrew?"

"Three C, across the hall."

"Thanks."

I could hear shoes moving away.

Six minutes.

I scrambled for the bathroom then. Found those pink, French-cut panties, zipped down my jumpsuit, and tucked them into my own underwear.

Couldn't afford a bulge in any pocket. Someone might notice and ask, and nothing good would result from that.

But I had to have something else to bring back with me. Some piece of evidence that I'd been here, and that proved I could carry something back with me through time.

I debated this longer than I'm proud of. I'd been so focused on finding those panties that I hadn't thought about the official reason for the mission, and what I'd need.

I almost grabbed a dozen things. My toothbrush. Used dental floss. A slice of bread.

In the end, I grabbed a dirty sock from out of my laundry. I might have noticed my toothbrush or some food going missing – and nobody would want to preserve my used dental floss for posterity as evidence of our success at time travel – but no way I'd notice a missing sock.

Like any sane person, I'd assume it was eaten by the washing machine.

I'd just stuffed the sock into the pocket of my jumpsuit when the time travel sensation overtook me.

TIME TRAVEL WAS UNLIKE ANYTHING ELSE I'D EVER EXPERIENCED, AND I'd trained as an astronaut.

The sensation began with floating. Not just in my gut, where I usually noticed that kind of kinetic sensation, but all through my torso, from, well, my bottom end all the way through my collarbone.

Then my head felt compressed, like when my big brother used to get me in a headlock and I managed to keep the pressure off my neck. It was that same squeezing from the sides.

But that wasn't just my head, getting squeezed that way. My hands and feet too. As though all my most distant parts got slowly crushed.

Then the squeezing moved inward, up my legs and arms, down my neck and shoulders, until every part of me felt compressed. As though time were a giant snake, trying to digest me.

All of this, while still getting that floating, weightless sensation.

But once those two sensations came together, then it got really weird.

For an instant, I could see everything. I mean everything. It was like every single thing around me was still connected to every single thing it had ever been and would ever be. I could see the flames that would consume this building someday. I saw the forest that once stood on this spot, and every tree connected to every board and every plank of wood ever to come into this building. Every cotton shrub that produced the clothes worn here, and everyplace those clothes would go, and every person who would wear them.

All of it. And so very much more.

Overwhelming.

I blacked out again. Just the way I had while traveling backward.

But that was the thing about time travel. That blackout might have lasted a year and a day, as far as my body was concerned. Only the doctors would be able to figure that out after I got back to my own time.

But in the moment, that blackout took exactly zero time.

It was as though the whole process, from the first hints of floating and compression through that instant of omniscience and my blacking out, all happened in less than a blink of my eyes.

At the end of that blink, I was still strapped to the white table, the I.V. tube still in my arm as though my body had never gone anywhere.

All around me, my team. Four of the best quantum physicists every assembled. Hyun Lee over working the keyboard of the temporal asymptote adjuster. Zamir, calibrating the tachyon relays with those four joysticks. Dottie, her pen light contrasting sharply with the dark skin of her hand, staring intently at my pupils. And Rodrigo, our team leader, overseeing the whole thing and checking everyone's work.

"He's here all right," Dottie said, her slow southern drawl making those words feel as though they took forever. Or maybe it was just an aftereffect of the time travel. "Like he's never been away."

"Better be here," Zamir said, and Hyun Lee echoed the sentiment. Zamir continued, "All readings show the drop and spike that correspond with our predictions."

"Yes," Hyun Lee added. "Everything has responded as though it worked perfectly."

"Well," Rodrigo said, giving me that slow smile of his. "Did you make it?"

"Yep. Right to my backyard, just the way we planned it."

That got everyone over to the table. Dottie and Zamir got the straps undone while Rodrigo popped my I.V. out and slapped a band-aid on the puncture point.

"Well?"

I'm pretty sure everyone asked that question at the same time.

I slowly stuck my hand into my pocket, ready for the big, dramatic reveal.

But my pocket was empty.

They must have seen it in my face. Or maybe in the way I was digging around in the pocket of my silver semi-cotton jumpsuit.

They all looked crestfallen.

"No," I said, sitting up. "I was there. I swear it. There was even a resonance effect we hadn't planned on. I could taste what I was having for dinner. I mean the me that lived through last week. His dinner. I could taste it from my backyard."

"And what did you try to bring back?" Rodrigo said, not trying to disguise the disappointment in his voice, but maybe holding out just a little hope.

"A dirty sock."

That got a general rumble of agreement about my choice.

"Oh, well," Rodrigo said. "We'll have to write this off as a failure and start troubleshooting what went wrong."

"No!" I jumped to my feet then on the black and white tile floor. "I'm telling you I was there. I saw Simone come into the backyard to do her yoga."

That got a snicker out of Zamir, but that was only because he'd met Simone a couple of times when he'd come over for a beer. Not because he had any idea about the night of absinthe and regret.

"There to watch, her, huh?" he said.

"No! It was as far back as we could send me. I just wanted to slip in through my back window and grab a sock and…"

"Doesn't matter," Hyun Lee said. "It's not evidence. Zamir already told us that Simone does yoga in the backyard every Thursday."

"Why do you think I always want to come over for a drink on Thursdays?" Zamir bobbed his eyebrows.

I shook my head. The team started to shut down the equipment.

"Wait!" I said.

"Just put it in your report," Rodrigo said. "We might be able to get some value out of your experience, at least, even if it was illusory."

"No! Wait!" Maybe it was the urgency of my tone, but they all turned and looked back at me. "My neighbor. Andrew. He had a visitor that night who tried to knock on my door. If I can confirm that – and I hadn't known it before – then that's new information I could only have gained by going backwards in time."

"Thin," Hyun Lee said.

"Too thin," Dottie added. "No way for us to prove you didn't already know."

"I spoke to him. The visitor."

"What?" Rodrigo's voice came out so sharp I half expected he'd cut my cheek.

"Through my front door. He'd tried to open it. He never saw me. And I gruffed up my voice so it didn't sound like me."

Rodrigo bobbed his head back and forth while he thought about that.

"Zamir," he said, "you go over to Jason's for a drink on Thursdays, right?"

Zamir nodded. "Not every Thursday, but yeah."

"So you have an excuse to be there. You ask the neighbor about it. Record the conversation. Video, if you can sneak it."

"Not legal," Dottie said in a sing-song tone.

"It's not evidence in court," Rodrigo said. "We just need proof for our records."

The two of them began to argue about that, while Hyun Lee and Zamir pressed me for everything I could remember about the trip through time. From the physical sensations, to the odd déjà vu bit, to the co-locative sense of taste and more. Everything I could remember.

Everything I admitted to remembering anyway. Because I could remember that night full well. Both my recent trip back, and the night I'd lived through.

I'd moved through time and space to try to spare Julie that discovery. Maybe I was being selfish, trying to keep Julie as my girlfriend even though I'd cheated, but I didn't see it that way. I saw it as trying to make up for one night's mistake. To save our relationship.

Didn't matter which way I thought of it though.

I failed to steal the panties from the past.

Julie found them that night. Knew they weren't hers.

We still had that fight.

Julie still dumped me.

Everything happened just the way I remembered it.

THE GOLDEN PEOPLE OF BELOWWORLD

Like a lot of writers, I read broadly. Not just in terms of genre, but in terms of time. In fact, I went on a "golden age of science fiction" kick a while back. Classics of the genre that hadn't been new since my parents were children.

(I feel another such kick coming on, too. Maybe it's time I finally re-read the *John Carter of Mars* stories, for the first time in about forty years.)

That spate left me thinking a lot about lost world stories. The kinds of stories where some explorer or adventurer finds a route to a seemingly different world, just inside the earth's crust (or similar).

I had to write one of these stories, as a kind of firebreak for my imagination. If I didn't, before long I'd end up writing a six-volume series about them or something. And that would interfere with the several series I have going now.

So, with any luck, this is an isolated story. But you never know...

The place was called Wizard Island. Of course I expected something strange.

Oh, I knew it was just a name. It went with Witches Cauldron, the cone of a long dead volcano, on an island in the middle of Crater Lake, Oregon. Still, I came down here hoping to find a sign of something unusual, and what I had in mind was a Bigfoot.

If you look at all the Bigfoot sightings reported in North America, the greatest concentration is around Crater Lake. Made sense then, for an amateur cryptozoologist like me to take his precious time off from graduate studies in Anthropology at the University of Oregon and come down here to camp and look for something wonderful.

God knows I needed a little wonder in my life. I'd just lost out on a summer internship in Prague, and my girlfriend Shirley had left me only two weeks earlier.

Our problem was a basic, scientific incompatibility. Shirley was a physicist, and after nearly six months together, she told me she could no longer see herself dating anyone who practiced a "soft" science.

As though anthropology was any less a science than physics. We all followed the scientific method, we all submitted our work for peer review. We all...

Still a bit sore, that wound. It was all I could think about that day, hiking around the dry dirt and scattered Douglas firs on Wizard Island. Well, almost all I could think about. As I said, I was hoping to find traces of a Bigfoot. Something I could apply the scientific method to and prove was real evidence. Something that would stand up to peer review. Something that would make the name of Andrew Warcrest mean something.

Maybe even something that would make Shirley realize she'd made a mistake.

Oh, I didn't want her back. No way. Once dumped, twice shy, as the saying goes. But I did like the idea of Shirley realizing she'd made a mistake. Crawling back to me on her hands and knees, begging for one more chance before I sent her packing.

Never happen, Shirl. Never happen.

Anyway, I'd snuck out here in my kayak during the predawn light, because the public isn't allowed on Wizard Island during the spring-time. Only during the summer. I figured that meant I'd have a better chance of finding my Bigfoot.

What I didn't figure was that it also increased my chances of finding rain.

I was somewhere around halfway up the seven hundred foot summit of that dead volcano, well away from the two official hiking routes, when spring clouds that had looked so innocent only a few minutes before, opened up.

And in Oregon, that really meant something. Oregon didn't get the kind of rain I saw growing up in the San Francisco Bay Area. Down around the Bay, rain came in dribs and drabs, spits and spurts.

But up here in Oregon, it knew how to *rain*.

Still, I was an Oregonian now, and I knew how to dress for that kind of rain. I was decked out in my good Columbia Sportswear rain gear, backpack and hiking boots, so I was dry everywhere but my face and hands in the warm, spring downpour.

No, the problem wasn't that the rain was getting *me* wet. The problem was that it was taking all that good, dry ground on the side of that cinder cone and rapidly turning it into slippery mud. Not just enough mud to ruin any potential Bigfoot tracks here. This was enough mud to make me seriously worry about my ability to get back.

I was a good hiker. I was in the right gear. But I was in the wrong place. A fire over the winter had cleared too much of the under-growth. The root systems that might normally have saved me weren't there.

The hillside around me grew slipperier and slicker by the moment, while the downpour filled the air with that wet mud smell.

I managed three safe steps down the slope – which meant I only needed to do that another hundred-odd times to reach the flatish section of the island, where the roots of the Douglas firs would hold the ground together and keep erosion from burying me – when it happened.

My feet went right out from under me. Slammed me down in the mud, and I started sliding. I dug my hands into the mud, desperate to at least control my slide, but hard as the rain was coming down, that dry dirt was soaking it up. And turning into slick mud. Everywhere my hands grabbed, they came up slimy and loose. Even the little bits of grass here and there did me no good. They came out by their roots.

All I could do was try to angle myself straight and hope for the best.

I was only maybe a hundred and fifty feet from safe ground when my feet found a crack. An actual, honest-to-God groove in the ground. Deep enough for me to jam my boots in, and rocky enough for them to stay. I locked my feet in place, determined to try to catch my breath. Get my heart rate down a bit and get some control of my situation.

Unfortunately, that crack was wider than I knew. And under just enough topsoil that the erosion happening around me opened it wide.

Wide enough to suck me inside.

Inside a cave. Not much of a cave, but more than enough for me to fall into. Landed on rock where mud and rain were coming in all too quickly. Walls were tight around me. I lay nearly perpendicular to the side of the dead volcano.

I scrambled to my slippery feet, finally sliding my feet out wide until they braced against the side of the little groove in the volcano. Too small now for me to think of it as a cave.

I blinked away sweat and rain. Dug a flashlight out of my green rain jacket. Clicked it on.

All igneous rock, far as I could tell. Geology was never my strong suit. And not much to see here anyway. Just a place to catch my breath for a moment, before I figured out how to...

Wait...

There, just about waist level. A cave drawing?

Couldn't be. Had to be graffiti. If there'd been a cave drawing here in Oregon, there was no way I'd have been lucky enough to be the first one to find it.

Still, I crouched down and looked closer. It was about at waist height. Sure looked like ochre for the ink. And the shape of the drawing, vaguely like a sun.

I traced the primitive corona and thought about how much I'd love to see the sun right that moment. How much I wanted to get out of this rain. How much I…

A deep rumble within the rocks slammed that line of thinking shut. Replaced by worry. If this was an earthquake, I was about to die. No way I wouldn't end up buried under even more mud than was already pouring in.

But the mud level seemed to stop rising, even as the rumbling continued.

Then the rock wall in front of me fell away, down to form a walkway through the dark rock. Mud didn't seem to flow down that walkway either, but it guttered off through a series of small drains, unless I was mistaken.

No idea how this was happening, but I wasn't going to question it. I hustled down that walkway, deeper into the volcano. A hundred yards. Two hundred yards. Three hundred, just to judge my counting my steps. The air should have been getting stale, but if anything it tasted fresher. It didn't taste of mud and rain, but carried almost a spring air scent. Like fresh grass and trimmed trees.

I don't think I was running exactly parallel to the ground either, but at a bit of a downward slope. Which just made me wonder all the more about those drains. They must have been well-designed, to keep this walkway so free of rain and mud. The only signs of either I could see were what I brought with me.

I was walking backwards, checking to see if I was assessing this right, when I fell again.

Down and down and down I slid, though a dark channel. Smooth as glass – some volcanic effect no doubt – and every moment I slid I seemed to go faster and faster. The air around me warmed quickly, and soon I was sweating in all my gear.

But finally the chute ended.

I landed in the middle of a gigantic fern.

Under a bright blue sky.

I blinked and blinked, but the scenery didn't change. I was lying on my back in a giant fern plant, here at the side of a cliff. Around me grew a forest of Douglas firs, hundreds of feet tall, complete with undergrowth.

And above those trees, a bright blue sky. And a yellow sun. Without any sign of clouds.

Must have been the scientist in me, but the moment I saw that sun I didn't ask questions. I just looked at my shock-proof, waterproof digital watch.

A little before noon. Which meant that sun was in the right position.

I pulled myself to my feet, and saw that a trail meandered through the woods from this fern plant. The soil was dark and rich, no doubt full of nutrients as volcanic soil often was. I looked up the red cliff side – which didn't look at all igneous, but dry, and more like something I would have expected to see in the southwest – and saw the opening I must have come flying out of.

So at least there was a connection. If I was dreaming – and right then I was pretty sure I was – at least my dream felt *somewhat* consistent.

I could hear birdcalls in the distance, but not ones I recognized. I could hear the buzz of insects too, which was weird for spring. But then, it was warmer down here than spring in Oregon. Warm enough I had to open my rain jacket and let some air reach the olive green, sweat-soaked tee shirt I wore underneath.

Didn't do much good. No breeze to speak of.

Well, there was no way I was climbing back up to that chute, so I started to hike down that trail. It twisted and turned through the trees, and every few hundred yards it intersected another trail. But those trails weren't at ninety degree angles, and this trail seemed to be going straight out from the cliff side. Which meant I was going to stick with the trail I had. Figured my chances were better of finding my way back.

Just to make sure, I pulled my compass out of a jacket pocket.

The needle spun and spun, and showed no sign of finding a true north.

That was more disturbing than I wanted to think about.

Being a scientist, though – no matter what Shirley thought – I did think about it. I must have run through a dozen hypotheses in my head when I heard the scream.

A woman's panicked scream.

I didn't even stop to think. Didn't even wonder how another person could have been down here. I just turned and started running.

And I did have to turn. That scream came from somewhere off to my left. Off my safe trail. But in the moment, I didn't care.

I had to crash through a dozen paces of underbrush before I reached a side trail that seemed to be going the right direction. I did find a branch of dead wood big enough to serve as a walking stick. Or in this case, maybe a thumping stick.

The scream came again, and this time I would have sworn it was a word.

"Nilixan!"

Not a word or a language I recognized, but I didn't waste time thinking about it. I doubled my pace on tired legs, determined to help whoever was in trouble.

As I came around the next bend, I saw the situation.

A beautiful woman. Small. Maybe five feet, which made her more than a foot shorter than me. Golden skin and long, blue-black hair. Apart from the staff in her hands, she wore only a loincloth. To be honest, her generous proportions might have distracted me if not for one thing.

Her face was contorted in panic.

But her wild eyes held challenge. And that staff in her hands was not just a walking stick. It had leather straps tied to both ends, with bits of skin and feathers bound to them, and two grips for her hands. She held the staff in a fighting grip, and looked like she knew how to handle it.

But she was outnumbered, and her enemies weren't human.

They looked like small velociraptors. Maybe four feet tall, with crests like some lizards have. They had her surrounded. More than a half dozen of them, and they were harrying her with pack tactics. Feinting in from one side, while the real attack came from the other.

She was holding her own pretty well, blocking each feint and still holding off the attacker, but her arms shook, like fatigue was setting in. And these lizards looked patient enough to wear her down before finishing her off.

Not if I could help it.

I dropped my backpack, screamed a challenge, and threw my legs forward in a mad dash, even as my own fatigue burned at my legs.

I got their attention though. Half the pack turned to look at me, and the woman took advantage of that opening to crack a skull.

Then I reached them, staff held low. I barreled through two of them, breaking necks, before they pack could adjust.

One of them darted in and caught me by the calf. Sharp pain spiked up my leg. It started twitching. I screamed in defiance and swung my club like a baseball bat. Cracked two skulls.

The woman had accounted for two more of her own by then, and the last couple of velociraptors, or whatever they were, fled into the forest.

My leg collapsed under me. I fell hard to the dark soil. I could taste something foul in my mouth. Tried to spit it out, but my lips felt puffy. I had to keep blinking. The light was so bright. So ... bright...

I DON'T HOW MUCH LATER IT WAS WHEN I AWOKE, BUT I WASN'T ON A trail anymore. I was in a small hut. The sides and top looked like lizard hide – dinosaur hide, maybe, if there were more of those velociraptors around. The air was sultry, and smelled of herbs and meat.

In the center of the small hut, the woman tended a fire, and had a cooking pot suspended above it. She scattered crushed leaves into it, muttering something I couldn't quite hear and definitely couldn't understand.

I tried to sit up, but that wasn't an option. My body felt like someone had filled my veins with lead. Moving took way too much effort. And my mouth tasted drier than a hangover, and about as fresh.

I must have made some noise, trying to get a little saliva going, because the woman turned and smiled at me.

Her smile was like sunrise after a storm. I felt lighter, safer, and happier just looking at that smile. Her features were odd, though. Symmetrical enough, but flatter than I was used to seeing, and her golden skin and orange eyes were tones I'd never seen on a human before.

The smile also made me acutely aware of how naked she was from the waist up.

I blushed and looked away, which got a puzzled sound from her.

"Fola neesa ishka nas?" she said.

"I'm sorry," I said, dragging my hand up to point to my ear, and still not quite looking at her. "I don't understand."

Odd as it seemed, she switched to Spanish. I'd had just enough Spanish to meet my language requirement, which meant I understood her, even if her accent sounded archaic to me.

"Do you thirst?"

I tried to nod, but my head began to spin and I said, "Please," instead.

She passed me a ceramic bowl full of water.

It tasted wonderful.

Now, I'm accustomed to good water in Oregon, but this was better than any water I'd ever tasted. It was fresh and clear and sweet, and I couldn't drink if fast enough.

My taste buds didn't think so anyway. My throat had other ideas, and in moments I started coughing up that wonderful water.

"Slowly," she said as I sipped. "The venom is defeated, but you need rest."

I sipped again, then tried to ask a question, but while I tried to remember how to phrase it, the room began to spin and I blacked out.

When I woke later, I felt better. Not strong, not really, but at least as though the lead in my veins was gone. I could sit up in the empty hut. Empty except for me, the think reed blanket that covered me, the fire with its cook pot, and a bowl beside me.

My nose told me it had some kind of stew or soup, savory. I wolfed it down. It had some meat with the texture of chicken, but a flavor closer to beer. Odd. I didn't recognize some of the vegetables in it either. Only the carrots and turnips. But I finished it in short order, and my throat felt all the better for the hot liquid.

Of course, given the strong herbal taste of the soup, it might have had healing properties too. Speaking of healing, I checked my leg. My pantleg had been sliced neatly away from the bit wound, and it was wrapped in wet leaves. Some kind of poultice over the bite itself.

But the skin in the area didn't look red or swollen, so I figured the woman must have known what she was doing. Her people had probably dealt with those bites more than a few times.

I stood, tested my weight on the leg. It held, with only a little shakiness. It would do.

My head was now uncomfortably close to the roof of this hut, but I hadn't planned on staying in here anyway. Now that I was awake and sensible, I could hear the signs of activity outside.

I ducked under the hut entrance and stepped out into the dawning light of morning.

All around me were more of these golden skinned people, scores of them in a thriving village. All about five feet tall. All with the same blue-black hair, the same flat features, and the same amazing shape. Even the men were built like swimmers, with a little extra muscle. Any one of the people around me could have graced the cover of a magazine. And they all wore nothing more than loincloths.

And they were all looking at me with those dazzling eyes.

The woman I'd met on the trail came running up between other huts.

"Wait," she said, in Spanish. "Wait."

She stood between me and her fellows, as though I were in

danger. Or maybe as though her people were. Either way, she said, "Peace. No threat here."

"I understand," I said, in broken Spanish.

That got nods all around, and the villagers – because that was the only way I could think of them – went back to what they were doing. Some of them were making spears, others were cleaning some kind of boar, still others were weaving or throwing pots or any of the hundred tasks they probably did as though this were a normal day for them. Even if it was as far from a normal day for me as it could be.

The woman from the trail smiled at me again, and once more her smile was enough to give me a lift, and relax some of my tight muscles. This time, though, I wondered if that was just an effect of her smile or something more. Was this some kind of calculated effect? Who were these people?

Another dozen questions flitted through my mind in quick succession, and I couldn't help giving voice to them.

"Where am I?" was the first.

Unfortunately, it didn't make much sense to her, judging by her answer.

"Here."

Then she blinked quickly and tilted her head this way and that in a gesture I didn't recognize, but thought looked like realization.

"You are in Belowworld. You are from Aboveworld. Yes?"

I nodded.

"This place. You found by accident. Yes?"

I nodded again.

"You saved me. I thank you." She bowed from the knee up, going halfway to a kneeling position before righting herself.

"And you saved me," I said. "I thank you."

I tried to imitate her movement, but my joints were stiff.

I must have done a good enough job, though, because she nodded.

"You came by accident, but you are here. Do you wish to stay, or return?"

"I wish to return, with proof." I looked around, eyes wild for something to bring with me, anything I could use to back this up as more than a story.

But while I was looking around, I realized she was shaking her head, a sad look in her eye.

"No proof. What you brought, you go back with." She pointed to my backpack, and my jacket, which I only now realized I wasn't wearing. "The rest," – she twirled her finger, indicating the whole of her village as well as my improvised club – "must stay."

"But, but..." I was sputtering, and I knew it. But this place was an anthropologist's dream. There was no way I could just abandon all these findings. There was so much I wanted to know. So much I wanted to study.

"No," she said firmly. "You saved me. You may stay, or you may go back. But no ... proof."

I looked around me. Everyone here was in better shape than I was, but if I lived the way they did, I'd probably look good too. Probably be able to pull my own weight, given time, especially with my size advantage. I could learn their language. Maybe even find love with this woman whose smile so lifted my spirits.

But could I? Could I just leave behind everything I knew to learn a whole new way of life, and never say a word about it?

No. No, despite Shirley's insistences, I was a scientist first and foremost. Study was only half of my calling. I had to report my findings. I had to give evidence.

No matter how much I learned here, without the ability to report any of it, I'd go crazy.

I shook my head, feeling as hangdog in my shoulders as my face must have looked. Here I was in the kind of place I'd dream of finding, and I wasn't going to be allowed to bring back a scrap of evidence.

Well, that was what *she* thought.

There were dozens of huts between where we stood and the perimeter, and I couldn't even see the cliffs from where I stood, only more Douglas firs surrounding the village. I'd find something to bring back. Some way to prove the story I'd write up.

"I have to go back," I said.

I only just completed the sentence when I heard a rush of air. Felt a sharp pain in my neck.

The world started to spin.

I woke up on a dry rock, down by a large lagoon, on Wizard Island. I was maybe three hundred yards from the shore, where my kayak sat waiting, concealed among some shrubs. The sky above me was overcast, and darkening as though evening was coming on quickly. I could smell rain in the musty air, and my stomach rumbled as though that soup had been ages ago.

According to my watch it was three days after I'd started my hike, here on Wizard Island. Most of that had to have been in the Below-world. I just wasn't hungry enough to believe otherwise.

The poultice was gone from my leg, but the healing bite marks might have come from insect bites. My fingers found another spot like an insect bite, this one on my neck.

Probably a blowgun dart, with some kind of sleep poison. Something to make me portable before they dropped me off. Let them make sure I brought back no evidence.

I dug a chocolate protein bar out of my backpack. I had to get something into my system before I made my way back across Crater Lake in the dark, and maybe in the rain.

Three days were all I could afford to spend here. I had to get back to my life.

But I was coming back. Oh, yes. I'd found something much better than Bigfoot.

I'd do some homework first. Research. Find out who had been there before me. Who taught them Spanish.

And then I'd find that crack again. Find my way back to those golden people.

And when I did, next time, I'd bring back proof.

YOUNG MONSTER
HUNTERS IN LOVE

The craft of writing isn't something you finish learning. There's always more, so I continue to take classes from successful writers who have been doing this much longer than I have.

Every one of those classes has exercises where we work on specific techniques that I could go on about with great excitement, but would probably bore you to death. Like listening to a chef go on about the fine points of chopping technique, when all you really want is to eat the meal.

Suffice to say, those exercises have left me with a number of potential openings for stories. Some of them stick in my head enough that I need to know where the story is going.

This is one of those stories.

ROD BROUGHT HIS LOAD OF LAUNDRY INTO THE BEDROOM. BRENDA WAS already in her pink nightie, which might have been enough to make him drop the load of laundry to take up a different pursuit, except she was clipping her toenails.

In bed.

Again.

Rod almost said something. Almost started the fight they'd already had twice this month, even though it would have put the kybosh on pink-nightie activities for the rest of the week. Instead, he saw a possibility.

This might have been the best possible time to tell her about his day.

Rod dumped the load of tee shirts on the bed, and started sorting sports shirts from metal band shirts. As he checked the wear on his old Type O Negative concert tee, he started speaking in the most bored tones he could manage.

"New neighbor at the end of the block."

"Yeah," Brenda said, sending a snip of big toenail high into the air before it landed on their good purple sheets. "Saw the moving van. D'you check it out?"

"Yep." Rod decided the shirt was still in good shape – at least as good as the old Star Wars shirt he was wearing with his baggy gray sweats – so he whipped it through a quick triple fold, and laid it on top on a gray Monster Magnet shirt. "Vampires."

"What type?" *Snip.* Another clipping leapt through the air.

"Well, vamp*ire* really." Rod folded three Timbers Army shirts in quick succession, cursing the fates that she cut right to the one question he didn't want to answer. How did she always do that?

Rod cleared his throat, and tried to evade the question.

"Just the one. Figured we could handle her."

"What type?" Brenda looked up, a single blond eyebrow arched high. Suspicion in her clear blue eyes.

Rod got very interested in untangling a pair of Halestorm tee shirts that somehow got wrangled together in the dryer.

"Rod."

Rod could feel his neck getting warm. He pulled a Dr. Who shirt out of the laundry basket, which was all wrong. It should never have been in this load. He frowned at it, tried to let his irritation take some of the tremor out of his voice.

"Figured we could take her out this weekend." He shook out the shirt. Snorted and folded it anyway. "Maybe Saturday we—"

"Oh, you've got to be kidding me." Brenda set down the clippers. "It's a Carmilla, isn't it?"

There was no good way to tell Brenda that a sex vampire had moved in down the street. Hell, Rod had trouble talking about the new neighbor without excitement rippling through him. Carmillas just had that kind of effect on men.

"Just tell me you weren't alone with her," Brenda said.

Rod could feel the heat starting to spread out from his neck. Tried to smooth and fold a Trail Blazers shirt as though he hadn't heard her.

Brenda wasn't having it.

The sight of her kneeling on the bed in her pink nightie, blond locks cascading around her smooth shoulders, would normally have been the most pleasant part of his day.

Right now Rod couldn't look at her. Not directly. He ran his fingers around the bottom hem of the tee shirt, trying to stop parts of it from curling in and starting a wrinkle that would only get worse.

But he could still see Brenda out of the corner of his eye. She pointed those clippers at him like a knife. He could smell the lavender of her body lotion now, more was the pity.

"You have five seconds to start talking, mister."

"Brenda, I—"

"Were. You. Alone. With. Her."

"I ... I don't think so." Rod buried his face in the tee shirt. Spoke through it. "I don't remember."

Brenda yanked the tee shirt away from his face. But her tone when she spoke was controlled. Like fury hadn't *quite* gotten hold of her.

"I didn't hear that. Say it again."

His words came out a mumble. "I'm not sure. I don't remember. Exactly."

"Rod," Brenda said, and her voice carried the weight of doom.

And that was the worst of all. Yelling at him, he could have handled. Anger, disappointment, righteous indignation – any of these things would have been fine with him. But no, her voice as she spoke held all the finality of a hanging judge.

"You better tell me everything right now. And I do mean everything. Because if I even think you're lying to me, or holding anything back..."

Brenda let her words trail off, but only because they both knew where that sentence was going. Not divorce. Not with her running back to her mother. Not with any of the kind of threats that might have surfaced in any other kind of marriage. But then, Rod and Brenda had never exactly had a normal kind of marriage.

The two had run into each other five years ago, barely old enough to drink but out hunting werewolves in the woods around Monterey, California. They'd teamed up, nearly gotten themselves killed, saved each other's lives, and ... celebrated their survival together all that first night.

They'd been together ever since.

No, Brenda wasn't just worried that Rod had cheated on her. She was worried that he was compromised.

"I was out for my afternoon run with the new ankle and wrist weights. Covered about five miles, sticking to the slopes of the hills around here. Overcast and darkish, but it's October, so you expect that, you know? Even when it's not going to rain." Rod shrugged. "I didn't think about what an overcast sky might mean until I got back to our block."

Rod risked a glance at Brenda. She'd lowered the clippers, and was idly trimming her fingernails. Even though she'd already trimmed them. Just more parings to end up digging into his skin later.

Assuming Brenda even let him sleep in their bed tonight, which was not a sure thing.

"Saw the moving van outside the old Johnson place, and ... I don't know. I just got that feeling, you know? Two of the three stories of that house were basements. Easily two of the three thousand plus square feet, underground." Rod shook his head. "Maybe it was the dead-eyed look on the big, beefy moving guys. Maybe it was the European-style furniture. Every bit of it looked old and hand-carved."

Rod shook his head again. "I ... just got that feeling, you know?"

Brenda nodded, absently snipping a bit of thumb nail. She did know. It was the same for her. Neither of them could explain how they knew when they were near something that wasn't human, but they could always tell.

"So," Rod said, "I figured I'd do the neighborly thing and poke my head in to say hi."

Rod immediately regretted his choice of words, and could see Brenda start to frown, so he pushed on.

"She was already in the house, of course. Thick black curtains keeping out the day, but she had old-fashioned gas lamps going on a pair of chestnut end tables. She was evaluating the pistachio paint job Johnson did with his old living room like she was trying to figure out which artworks should go where..."

"Rod." Brenda snapped her fingers in front of his face. Great. His tone must have been getting dreamy. He knew his body was responding to the memory just as ... well, just the way it had responded to the sight of Brenda in her pink nightie.

"Name her," Brenda said, "and describe her."

"Veronique," Rod said, and he hated the teenager-with-a-crush tone in his voice, but he couldn't help it. "Model tall, with long raspberry hair trailing all the way down her back. She has the kind of curves that would get her a centerfold, but she hid them under a conservative, elegant dress with a high neckline. Burgundy. Set off her pale skin. She smelled like tulips."

"Eye color," Brenda said, tone all business. Clippers forgotten in her hand in much the way Rod had forgotten he was still holding that now-rumpled Trail Blazer shirt.

"Bl... no ... gr..." Rod scratched at the back of his neck, then ran his fingers up his scalp over the buzz cut of his brown hair. "I'm not sure."

"Where were the movers? Were any in the room with you?"

"I think so." Rod focused hard. "I remember them ... moving around..."

"What did her voice sound like?"

That question. That question was important, but at the moment Rod couldn't remember why. So he tried to remember. He'd introduced himself. She'd done likewise. Held out her hand and Rod ... Rod had kissed it, even though at the time it seemed weird to him...

"Honey," Rod said. "Her voice sounded like honey. Not in that southern drawl kind of way. It was more like..." – Rod grimaced as he only now realized exactly what his words meant, but he wasn't going to hold them back, not from Brenda – "like it dripped sweetness down my spine."

"Oh, Rod," Brenda said with a sigh in her voice. "Sweet Rod. She took you."

"No," Rod said, his whole face burning with a blush that belied his own memory. "I really don't think she did. I remember her talking about art, and ... and her laughter like crystal chimes..."

"And then you remember leaving, right?" Brenda shook her head. "But the movers. They were gone when you left. Weren't they?"

Rod focused hard. He'd remembered the sounds of the movers while he was talking to Veronique. Their heavy footsteps. Their quick words of coordination. The sounds of crates and furniture being set on hardwood floors.

He'd remembered seeing them in the background when he introduced himself...

"The van was gone." All the blood drained out of Rod's face. "I was only there a few minutes, but when I left the van was gone."

"Compromised." Brenda sighed and hopped off the bed to done her thick purple bathrobe. "If you're capable of acting under your own power, go sit in our bathtub right now. If not, my dearest Rod, you know what that means."

Rod's feet suddenly didn't want to move. He knew what was

coming. What had to happen next. Rod had to get in the tub. Had to. Had to wait there while she called Father Don. Had to sit still while they purged him of the Carmilla's taint.

But his feet didn't want to move.

"Honey," Brenda said, "get your sweet ass in that tub."

The room started spinning. Getting in the tub was bad. Getting in the tub would take away the honey dripping up and down his spine. Would take away the lingering taste of cinnamon pleasure on his tongue from…

Oh, God, he *was* compromised.

Rod started hyperventilating.

He got one foot in the air, but he couldn't set it down in the direction of the tub. He refused to set it back down where it had been though. He pushed and pushed to get moving.

In the background, he could hear Brenda on her cell phone. Knew who she was calling. Knew Father Don was coming. Rod had to act. Had to warn his mistress…

His mistress?

Rod got that foot down on the thin green carpet of his spinning bedroom, in what he thought was the right direction for his bathroom and their tub. Cold sweat drenched him now, stinging his eyes and plastering his shirt to his chest. His lungs were working triple time, and his heart beat even faster than that.

Too fast and too shallow. Too much conflict. The room spun faster and faster. Started going black.

The last thing Rod saw before he passed out was Veronique's face.

But his lips whispered Brenda's name.

FATHER DON WASN'T REALLY A FATHER, IN ANY SENSE OF THE WORD. HE wasn't a priest, officially, and he had no children, though that wasn't because of any vow of celibacy. His name wasn't actually even Don.

His name was Carmichael. But when he was growing up and showed that he had a gift for driving the bad feeling out of places, kids in the old neighborhood started calling him Don Carmichael out of respect. Then it was just Don.

When he went off to college and drove the poltergeist out of the Kappa Kappa Epsilon sorority house, the girls started calling him Father Don, though they giggled when they said it. And some of them offered him "confessions."

He found the whole thing funny enough that he got ministerial credentials from one of those mail-order churches, just in case anyone wanted him to perform a wedding.

Anyway, the nickname stuck. Helped that he liked to dress in black, and he had penetrating dark eyes and kept his black hair cut short. He looked lean, and every inch a man who should have been a priest and an actual exorcist, even though he could never have kept any one of those priestly vows.

He liked his bourbon, and he liked his women. But what he liked most of all was driving out the things that had no place pestering the good people of this world.

So even though it was almost midnight on a Friday night – and even though it meant sending home sweet Charlotte who liked to play "the innocent nun and the horny priest" before their game had really gotten underway – Father Don didn't hesitate to hop in his Civic and break more than a few speed laws to get to Rod and Brenda's house.

They had a nice two-story – which meant three-story if he included the basement – in the hills of southwest Portland, just a few miles up twisty roads from his place in Lake Oswego.

Brenda met him at the door, dressed for business. Her blond hair in a bun behind her head, and her fighting-trim body in kicking jeans and a Lycra top. She looked ready to kick ass, which was for the best, though Father Don did feel a little disappointed.

When she'd called, she'd said something about them getting ready for bed when trouble hit, and, well, Father Don had been hoping to catch a glimpse of her in something a little slinkier.

Brenda gave him a quick, one-armed hug and ushered him straight upstairs.

"What are we dealing with?" Father Don asked as he quick-stepped through the bedroom to the closed door of their master bathroom. "You only said—"

"To get here A.S.A.P. Yeah." Brenda grimaced. "A Carmilla got him. Just this afternoon."

"A Carmilla?" Father Don didn't try to keep the tremor out of his voice. Brenda would have expected it anyway. His ... appreciation of the female form made him even more susceptible to Carmillas than most men. "Where?"

"End of the block. The old Johnson place."

"I'm not sure—"

"Look." Brenda grabbed Father Don's shirt in a clenched fist and pulled him down to eye level with her. "Right now that bitch has her hooks in my Rod. *You* are going to unhook him. Clear?"

"So you don't need me to—"

She pulled him nose to nose. "I said, 'clear?'"

"Clear," Father Don croaked, then swallowed hard.

Brenda let go of his shirt, and opened the door.

Rod was sitting naked in the bathtub. Not a sight Father Don wanted to see, all the more because Rod had the kind of lithe, rippled muscles that made even a guy in decent shape like Father Don feel inadequate.

But Rod had that look in his eyes. Like a love-struck puppy, and he wasn't making googly eyes at his hot wife which was as good an indicator as any that Brenda had done the right thing to call him.

Father Don sighed and stepped across the white linoleum floor to the white marble double sink and began washing his hands.

"Father Don," Rod said, "this is all a misunderstanding. I'm sure I wasn't alone with Veronique for more than a moment."

"Really," Father Don said. "So why do you smile when you say a vampire's name?"

Rod didn't have an answer for that, but Father Don wasn't listening anyway. Washing his hands right now was too important a ritual. As he scrubbed the foam over every inch of his fingers, hands and wrists, so too was he cleansing himself of distraction and impurity.

By the time he was done, it could have been Brenda sitting naked in that tub, and Father Don wouldn't have even stolen a glance.

"Close the door," he said to Brenda.

She did, but she was on the inside. She intended to stay for this then.

"Over here," he said to her. And she joined him over by the sinks. He pointed at her reflection. "What do you see?"

"Don, we don't have time for—"

"Answer the question."

Brenda glowered at him, then puffed out a breath and made a show of looking her reflection up and down.

"I see the woman who's going to kill the bitch who tried to ensnare her husband."

Father Don stepped up behind her. "Look into your eyes. What else do you see?"

"Get to the point, Don."

Father Don made her wait through a long, slow breath. The kind of relaxed breath she couldn't take right now. Not with that furrowed brow, all that tension through her shoulders, arms, and posture. Not when the only thing that kept her from pacing was the fact that he had her looking in the mirror.

And that wasn't all he could feel. Empathy, that was just one of his gifts.

"You're in pain. I understand that. And you're angry at Rod. I understand that too." He laid one gentle hand on her shoulder. "But you need to realize that whatever happened today, Rod didn't cheat on you."

"He—"

"He tried to check out a possible vampire and fell into a trap. He didn't go to her. She snared him. She didn't 'try' to ensnare him. She did it. *This is not his fault.*"

"I know he's the victim."

"Intellectually, yes." Father Don shook his head slowly so she could see it. "But I can feel the anger coming off you in waves. And the pain. And the sense of rejection."

Father Don leaned in and whispered, "But when we kill her, he will be himself again."

"I want him back *now*." Tears started streaming down her face. She had to lean forward on the counter with both hands as sobs wracked her. "I—"

"It's all right," Father Don said, but didn't embarrass her with shushing sounds. "Take as long as you want. But I needed you to break through the wall of anger if you're going to stay in here for this."

Brenda slipped down to her knees, crying. Father Don left her to gather herself and went back to Rod. Rod, who didn't even show an ounce of sympathy for the pain and tears of the woman he loved.

As though Father Don didn't have enough evidence of what was going on here.

"Stretch out, Rod." Father Don began rubbing his hands together.

"Father Don, this isn't necessary. Really. We just had a fight. She was cutting her toenails in bed again, so I made up some—"

"Silence!" Father Don said, putting all the authority he could muster into one word and letting it ring out.

Rod looked back at him, eyes slightly glazed, but hands coiled into fists.

"It's the taint of the Carmilla that puts those words into your mouth," Father Don said in a low voice. "The same taint that coils your fists in anger at me, and forces you to ignore your crying wife."

Rod opened his mouth to say something, but no words came out. Father Don almost sighed in relief. It was one thing to be able to call on that sense of Authority when confronted directly with something foul, but something only tainted?

That didn't always work when the foul thing itself wasn't present.

Father Don rubbed his hands together faster, muttering hopeful words to any gods or saints that might have been listening. As far as he could tell, no gods or angels seemed to be involved in what he did, but just asking for help seemed to kick his Authority up a notch. So even if that part was all in his head, Father Don kept doing it.

He could feel it now. Heat between his hands, spreading into an aura around him.

Brenda was back now, only a little redness in her eyes giving any hint of the tears she'd shed.

"Turn on the water," Father Don said. "Just a trickle."

Rod moved his feet out of the way while Brenda started the hot tap.

Father Don cupped his hands under the water letting them fill. He turned to Rod.

Rod kicked Father Don's hands, splashing the water over all of them.

Father Don ignored the water in his eyes and shoved his hot, wet hands against Rod's chest.

No words now. Just Authority. Just the aura surrounding Father Don, centering on his hands, shoving its way into Rod. Burning away anything that wasn't supposed to be there. Anything that wasn't Rod himself.

Rod screamed and thrashed. He tried to punch Father Don, but couldn't make himself do it. He might have kicked Father Don, but Brenda had his feet now, pinning them to the porcelain of the tub.

Rod must have banged his head against the tub a half-dozen times, but it couldn't be helped. All Father Don could do was hold his hands firm against Rod's strong chest, burning away the taint of the Carmilla.

Father Don could feel the progress of his Authority through Rod's system. Spreading first through his chest and torso, then up into his head, down through his arms. His legs next, then into his hips, and finally into his genitals.

Rod's screams hit a high note then, for most of the taint of a Carmilla was centered on the place of her greatest influence.

Finally, Rod collapsed.

Father Don collapsed too. Not unconscious, like Rod, but panting and sweating against the linoleum floor. His heart was going so fast it might have been beating for both him and Rod through the whole process.

His mouth was dry as it always was after channeling Authority, and he couldn't quite focus on what Brenda was saying to Rod as she stroked his unconscious forehead.

In fact, she had to repeat herself twice when she started speaking to Father Don, before he understood her words.

"He's free now, right?"

Father Don nodded.

"She has no more hold on him?"

"That's what free means." Father Don dragged himself to a sitting position, leaning against the white wall beside the fluffy teal towels. "We got to him in time to break the hold without permanent damage."

Brenda sat on the edge of the tub and looked Father Don over.

"You want a drink?"

"Bourbon, if you got it."

She was back pretty quickly with a bottle of Jack Daniels and two glasses with ice. Father Don barely had time to wash his face and hands, and get his breathing and heart rate under control.

She poured them each a double. They sat on the linoleum and toasted.

"To good friends," Father Don said.

They drank in silence for a moment. It was Gentleman Jack, which was a little higher class than their main line, but what mattered most was the bite of the bourbon on his tongue.

"I want her dead tonight," Brenda said. "I want her gone before she can steal anyone else's man."

"Better to wait until day, when—"

"It was day when she snared Rod. And from his description, she might have the movers half-under her control too. Tomorrow she'll have help. Right now she might be alone."

"Right now she'll be at the peak of her powers."

"But if we wait, we risk hurting innocent men to get at her."

Brenda shook her head. "No. We go in tonight. She won't be expecting it, and she's not likely to have live-in help yet."

That got a raised eyebrow out of Father Don.

"And what makes you say that?"

"She literally moved in today, but she still took a bite out of my husband." Brenda quirked a smile. "If she had a thrall, would she risk taking the first step with a married man in her new neighborhood?"

Realization washed over Father Don, and with it he could feel the ping of Authority. Whatever it was that let him do what he did, it agreed with Brenda.

"All right then. Let's finish our drinks."

"Then go finish her." Brenda was smiling now, but it was the smile of a cat about to pounce.

They finished their drinks and stood. Father Don pointed to Rod.

"Want me to help you get him to bed?"

"Let him sleep there tonight," Brenda said. "After all, he was stupid enough to go into a vampire's home without me."

THE OCTOBER AIR WAS COLD, BUT THEY WERE BETWEEN RAINS AT LEAST. And Brenda welcomed the cold. Maybe a bit of a shiver through her Lycra top, but it kept her alert. Made her aware of her skin, and then every sight and sound of the night.

Yellow-orange sodium dimly lit the quiet street. In this part of Portland, street lights were less frequent, and street repairs nearly as rare as unicorn sightings.

In her martial arts shoes, Brenda made little noise crunching gravel at the edges of the barely paved street. Alas, the same couldn't be said for Father Don, who crunched along as though this were a casual stroll through Riverfront Park.

That was the price of bringing Father Don, though. Well, that and his occasionally stealing glances at her ass. But when the Authority was flowing through him, nobody but Rod was better at her back.

And right now Rod was dead to the world, sleeping off the trauma to his soul.

Brenda didn't have Authority on her side though. But she had her thrice-blessed silver dagger, and a white hawthorn stake she'd cut and carved herself back when she was still a virgin.

That would have to be enough.

The old Johnson place was set back from the road behind a wild front yard. Douglas fir trees and Japanese maples, with undergrowth of Oregon grape vines and blackberry brambles. A simple white house practically set into its own private forest.

Long gravel driveway, and parked at the end – in front of the white, two-car garage – was a high-end Mercedes coupe.

"Alarms?" Father Don whispered.

"None," Brenda whispered back. "Johnson never believed in them. He kept Dobermans and a shotgun instead."

They crunched their way past the house and around toward the back door. Brenda knew that led into the kitchen. She glanced around to make sure no one was watching, but the fences in the backyard were high.

The backyard looked more suburban. Grass lawn with a hot tub and a big brick barbeque, and very tall redwood fences. No trees or garden though, which was just weird. Why cultivate the backyard and stop short of making it pretty?

Father Don pulled a set of lock picks out of his pocket and started on the back door...

But something was wrong with this. Brenda couldn't quite put her finger on what, but doing what she did meant listening to her intuition anytime it had something to say.

And it was talking loudly.

"Stop," she said.

Father Don stopped, but he didn't put his lock picks away.

"What's wrong?"

"I don't know," she said slowly, "but..."

Her eyes focused on the Mercedes.

"The garage," she said. "Why park that nice car in the driveway? Why not use the garage?"

"You think she's set up her lair in the garage?" Father Don shook his head. "But you said the Johnson place has two levels of basement."

Brenda shrugged. Started walking toward the garage. It had a side door toward the back, and a series of stepping stones that led to the house. Behind her she heard Father Don curse and hurry to catch up.

Brenda was just reaching for the door handle when the door opened with a long, slow creak.

A shiver made its way down Brenda's back.

The garage inside was lit to dim twilight, and it looked like the dream of some 70s sybarite. And the whole place smelled like sex.

Concrete floor covered with throw rugs made from animal hides; zebra, lion, and cheetah were the first three Brenda could pick out. Huge beanbag chairs in primary colors. Purple and red sheet curtains covering the walls where Old Man Johnson had kept his countless racks of tools.

Three red, fuzzy couches that were so deep and heavily cushioned Brenda doubted that even an Olympic athlete could get off of one without aid.

And on one side of the room, a heart-shaped bed covered in rumpled, pink silk sheets. A man with the build to be a middle linebacker lay passed out on that bed, next to a woman with long hair the color of raspberries. She was as naked as the man next to her, and Brenda felt a momentary twinge of envy over the perfection of the woman's body.

"Well," the Carmilla said in honeyed tones. "You must be Mrs. Rod. Thank you ever so much for sending over such a delightful ... package to welcome me to the neighborhood."

"Wrong, bitch," Brenda said. "You messed with Mr. Brenda, now I'm going to—"

"*And who,*" the Carmilla said loudly, "is that delightful morsel next to you? Oh, you *shouldn't* have."

Brenda gave up the verbal antics and started sprinting toward the vampire, weapons raised.

The Carmilla was on her feet before Brenda managed three steps.

And Father Don was still in the doorway.

Brenda knew that was the aura of a Carmilla. Knew that Father Don wouldn't be able to act until he got the Authority flowing through him. But still, she couldn't help muttering, "Men."

Brenda swung her dagger in a cut for that smooth belly, but the Carmilla vanished in a blur.

Left of Brenda.

No.

Past Brenda.

No.

All the way to the doorway.

Father Don was right. They should have waited until morning. The Carmilla was just too powerful while the sun was below the horizon.

Brenda was going to die tonight. Without ever getting a chance to tell Rod she loved him one more time. Without the chance to tell Rod she forgave him for getting ensnared by the Carmilla in the first place.

The hell with that.

Brenda slid across the zebra hide rug like she was stealing second to pop to her feet and start running back at the Carmilla before the damned thing enthralled Father Don.

Father Don, who was still stuck in the doorway. His lips moved in that non-prayer thing he did, looking for some kind of help to summon the power he couldn't quite control.

The Carmilla was talking to him. Using her voice to take the first stages of control of him, and already Father Don had a goofy smile spreading across his face. She was speaking French. The only word Brenda could pick out was her name: Veronique.

So Brenda went with that.

"Hey, Veronique!" she said as she came to a stop inside stabbing range. "Getting a little hefty in the hindquarters."

It was a lie, but it got her attention. Veronique turned with fury flashing in her eyes.

Brenda slashed out with her dagger. Trailed a line of blood across that perfect belly.

Veronique's long, blood red nails like talons as they seized Brenda around the throat. Crushing pain. Brenda started stabbing with her dagger, but her arms felt weak as soggy washcloths. She couldn't even tell if she struck home.

"Silver," Veronique scoffed. "The moon's metal is nothing to a creature born of the moon blood. Already your feeble scratches close. You are a fool, hunter."

Tighter, the Carmilla squeezed. Brenda felt her heart pounding in her chest and her pulse in her throat. The world was going red already. Her lungs fluttered, frantic for air.

"And you brought a man," Veronique continued. "What is a man to stand against me?"

"A man is nothing," Father Don said. "But Authority bows before no one."

And he put his hands on her shoulders. That was all. No sizzle of burning flesh. No angelic glow. No choirs of heavenly voices. Just his hands on the Carmilla's shoulders.

But the Carmilla dropped Brenda.

A momentary reprieve. Every instinct in Brenda's body and soul cried out that what Father Don had done was nothing more than a solid jab to the creature's power. That any moment it would rally, just as strong. Stronger, perhaps, in that it understood its enemies all the better now.

But Brenda denied it that moment.

With a scream of rage and defiance, Brenda dropped her silver dagger and plunged her hawthorn stake right through that perky chest and into the foul heart within. Father Don shoved the Carmilla forward from behind, adding just that little extra momentum to the strike.

The Carmilla exploded outward in a spray of blood. Drenching Brenda, Father Don, and the room itself. As though the creature were composed entirely of blood, and every cell of her erupted outward at the same time.

Brenda had to blink her eyes clear of blood before she could see anything, and the first thing she saw was a blood-covered Father Don doing the same thing.

"Did you know it was going to do that?" Father Don asked.

Brenda nodded. Held up the stake.

"Cut it myself when I was a virgin." Talking hurt her throat, and her words came out raspy. "Carmillas don't react well to that."

"You could have warned me," he said, pulling out a handkerchief and trying to clear his eyes and face.

"Didn't want you to hesitate," she said. "Any more than you did, I mean."

"Hey, it's not easy to attack a—"

"Yeah, yeah," she said, pushing past him to get out of the love nest.

"What about him?" Father Don asked, pointing at the guy who was – Brenda hoped – asleep in the bed.

"Let him sleep it off. With any luck, the blood will dissolve on its own. Sometimes it does. And he's not going to remember tonight clearly anyway."

Father Don nodded, but Brenda started walking. She wanted to get home and take a shower.

The blood might dissolve away on its own, but she wasn't going to wait for it.

Rod woke up alone in the bathtub. After a moment trying to remember who he was and where he was and why, it all snapped together in his head. He leapt up, threw on fighting clothes, grabbed a thrice-blessed silver dagger and a stake of black hawthorn and ran down the stairs...

Just in time to see his front door open and his gore spattered wife and friend come inside.

Rod grabbed Brenda in his arms anyway, and she gave him a tired but sincere hug.

"It's dead?" he asked.

"Nobody messes with my man," Brenda rasped.

Rod whipped off his Lycra shirt and wiped her mouth clean so he could taste her when he kissed her. She tasted of bourbon, but she kissed him back like she hadn't seen him in weeks.

That kiss lasted through Father Don saying something about laundry and a shower.

The kiss went on and on for some time, and when it finally finished, Brenda said something about a shower and about twelve hours' sleep.

Rod wondered how well she'd sleep with those toenail parings in their good purple sheets, but decided not to say anything.

In fact, he resolved not to complain about Brenda cutting her toenails in bed anymore...

Well, for a while, anyway.

FLINGING THE DOOR OPEN

Writing can carry with it a certain amount of catharsis. Frustrations, angers, disappointments, sadness ... all these things and more can power fiction. Sometimes that means actually taking what's upsetting the writer and fictionalizing it.

More often though, at least for me, it means taking the emotions involved and letting them carry the story in the directions it wants to.

Sometimes, that can lead to intense thrillers. Other times, there can be sweet poignancy. And somewhere in between, there's this story.

I was righteously angry when I wrote it, though not for reasons that could be discerned through reading this story. No thinly veiled facts here. Just raw, real emotion that underwent an interesting change for me in the course of the story.

(And if you're wondering, yes, I'm fine.)

THERE'S POWER IN PAIN.

That was the lesson my master never taught me. Then again, what should I have expected from a guy who wanted me to call him "master" in the early part of the twenty-first century? Every time I said it, I felt as though I should have topped it off with an Igor accent, like some reject from an off-off-off-brand *Frankenstein.*

Then again, my master was teaching me magic in modern-day Portland, Oregon, so maybe a term of respect wasn't half the reason I sometimes felt like a reject from the late late show.

Yeah, yeah, magic is real. I'm sure that blows your physics-laden mind. Like half the freaking country doesn't have superstitions or other odd beliefs. Just watch sports fans get ready for a game. Then tell me no one believes in magic anymore.

Sorry. When I get hurt I lash out. And pain was the whole point of this, wasn't it?

My master, he taught me to find moments of power in joy. In laughter. In delighted surprise. Very New Age in his approach, even if his ideas and techniques were very old.

And they worked.

Not movie-special-effects kind of magic, but the more important kind. The kind that got my Lit prof to give me an extension on my mid-term paper, against all warnings and policies. The kind that got gorgeous Jenny Coulson to notice me even though she had been fixated on…

Well, that guy's name doesn't really matter.

And yes, I only mean "notice." Yes, I could have used magic to punch her interest up a few notches – or something more than that – but that's never been the kind of guy I am.

In general, I like having magic open doors for me. Always figured if I couldn't handle the rest, then I was a pretty sorry individual.

And Jenny Coulson is still my girlfriend two years later. So I'd like to think that says something good about me.

Anyway, Jenny wasn't the reason I was in pain. That was a college friend. Stu Reinhold. I figured Stu and I were just about as close as two friends who lived on opposite ends of the country could be.

When I had doubts about my career as a painter – the kind who gets gallery shows, not the kind who does the trim on your house (not that there's anything wrong with that) – Stu was there to tell me I had talent. I had drive. I had everything it took to make it in my chosen profession.

When Stu was having troubles with his girl, Allison, I was right there on the phone talking him down, then talking him through it.

I thought we were good friends.

It was at that convention when I found out I was wrong.

The convention was up in Seattle, the brainchild of a couple of *Star Trek* fans that exploded into a major annual event. I was up there to see Stu and to try to get some book cover commissions.

Stu was there to make business contacts on the video game front. And apparently that was it.

We were supposed to room together. Room 506 at the Sheraton. Set up months in advance.

I got there to find out my double had become a single. Stu was in a suite of his own now. Even left me a voice mail to say, "We should try to catch dinner while we're both here though. Or maybe lunch. Dinners are big business, and—"

I was standing in the Sheraton lobby when I got that message. Me and five thousand strangers in various stages of checking in or heading for the conference rooms. Some in costume, others like me in jeans and geek-stamped tee shirts, even a few in suits, and all of them turning the air conditioned hotel lobby into a near-sweltering sardine can where apparently deodorant was optional.

I'd arrived smiling, with that flutter of excitement I always get when I get together with friends. So much to talk about. Maybe the chance to help each other with contacts, introduce each other to people we knew. I was an artist, but Stu was a business major. Usually made for good cross-focus introductions.

Most of all, I wanted to just catch up and renew ties.

But all those ties severed in a single phone message.

I didn't even listen to the end of it. What was the point? This was supposed to be the two of us taking on the convention. That was how we'd talked about it. Instead, I was just another contact. Just another business meal, and not even important enough for a dinner.

Ever have one of those moments where – in the flash of a single second – you see an entire cross-section of your past in a new light?

I'd made a bunch of friends at U.O. Or so I'd thought at the time. But really, in that one moment, I realized that I only talked to those friends when *I* called *them*. Never the other way round. If they passed through Portland, I heard about it later, with apologies that, on social media, might have been sincere.

I'd assumed they were.

In that one moment, that one flash, I realized that maybe they weren't.

I was the shy kind of kid, growing up. Never had an easy time making friends, and the few I made I held onto for dear life. I'm still close with them.

In college I tried to change the shy part. Tried to open up. Tried to make myself meet more people. Make more friends.

Turns out, all I'd made were acquaintances.

Including Stu.

As I stabbed my phone to hang up, to cut off that hell-spawned message, I saw it all clearly for the first time. How wrong I'd been about Stu. About everyone I met in college. Everyone except Jenny. But I didn't think about her. Not in that moment. I thought about Stu, and Mary, and Allison, and Jake, and the rest of the gang.

All a lie.

And the pain of it wracked my system. My guts cramped like the time I'd drunk sour milk on a dare in grade school. I felt like a cold weight settled in over my whole body, pushing from the shoulders down.

I could feel my skin. I mean all of it. Like the air wasn't flowing with the air conditioning system, but hovering around me, afraid to touch the pariah.

No tears though. When I look back, that's the strangest thing. The most painful social moment for me since high school, when the girl who took my virginity dumped me two days later for some basketball player, but I didn't cry.

I didn't think about tears then, though. As I hung up my phone, all I thought about was the pain. The lurching thump of my heart. The weirdness of my skin.

And underneath it all, the flare of power.

Lots of power.

***

I WAS A COLLEGE FRESHMAN WHEN I MET MY MASTER. EIGHTEEN AND wide-eyed, pushing myself to do new things. To meet new people. I took every flier people handed me, and I made myself smile and thank them. I read every flier stapled to telephone pole or tacked up on a bulletin board.

I had plans to join four or five clubs that first semester. Maybe get involved in campus politics. Having to give speeches in public sounded like the best way to get over shyness that I could think of. So many possibilities...

I shuffled my stack of fliers and pulled one out at random.

It was pale blue. Had a big, black triangle on it, and inside the triangle it read, simply, "Destiny is a ship, not a destination. Learn to take the rudder. Six p.m. sharp. Tonight." After that, just an address, off-campus.

Not the kind of thing I would have done, but that was the whole point. Obviously I had to go.

I tried inviting my roommate and the guys next door, but they thought it sounded like some self-help crap. Tony Robbins stuff. I almost agreed with them, except that they couldn't see the triangle. I'd shown the flier to all four, and each time I asked what the triangle meant. Each one said the same thing: "What triangle?"

That settled it for me. I was too intrigued to not show up. So at six o'clock that night, according to my phone's clock, I knocked on the door of that address. A purple door on a yellow house that, from the front, didn't look like it could have held more than a single bedroom, despite the third-acre lot surrounding it.

The house, like the flier, was more than it seemed. But I didn't know that yet.

The door was opened by a slender old man. The kind of old man I wanted to be when I grew up. He was shorter than me, but his movements were lithe and smooth. Graceful, even. He had a full head of salt-and-pepper hair, tied back in a ponytail. His eyes were the color of caramel. He had only a few wrinkles, all smile and laugh lines. He wore a faded black linen shirt and faded black linen slacks that both looked ridiculously comfortable. His feet were bare.

He looked like a martial artist. A Tai Chi master, maybe. That was my first impression, anyway, and I turned out to be not far off.

"Tell me," he said in a clear, high voice, "did you see anything but words on the flier that brought you here?"

"A big, black triangle."

He nodded. "And what time did you knock?"

"Exactly on time?"

"Indeed." He smiled then, and those caramel eyes almost lit up with the smile. I felt better just talking to him. He stepped aside and swept his arm back in a gesture of welcoming.

I was the only one who'd found the flier. The only one who "was supposed to" he'd said that day, and it wasn't until later that I realized how right he was. He'd cast a spell for an apprentice, and I'd answered.

I didn't join any clubs that semester, or go into campus politics. I didn't care though. I was too busy.

I spent hours with him every week. Studying, meditating, and practicing. I may have majored in the fine art of painting, but I minored in magic.

It was my master's tutelage that helped me define the ethic of my magic. Never too much. Only enough to open a door. Walking through should be done on one's own.

And I never considered violating that ethic. Not until years later.

Not until I got dumped by a friend via voice mail.

Moments of power happen every day. They happen to everyone. Little ways we get jarred out of the mundanity of life. Magic is the art of noticing those moments. Of snatching them before they pass, and turning them to the magician's own purposes.

Not all of them, of course. Only a few.

For a normal person, those moments flit passed unnoticed and fade into the background before they have a chance to create any kind of real, lasting change.

But for a magician – I refuse to call myself a wizard, even though my master called our art "wizardry" – a single snatched moment becomes infinite.

Snatching a moment stops it. Stops time. Stretches it out until the magician sets that moment free, carrying with it a spell powered by the emotion of that moment.

The first time Jenny said she loved me, that moment powered a spell to get us a fantastic vacation deal in Tahiti. I admit though, I held that moment longer than I needed to, letting myself revel in the moment. The amazement that a girl as wonderful as Jenny could love a guy like me. The warm perfection of realizing my own love for her was returned.

I lingered in that moment before releasing it with a spell.

But at that convention in Seattle, standing there in the Sheraton lobby and nearly overwhelmed with pain. Part of my mind recognized the power of that moment.

And I snatched it.

I gripped it tight, but I didn't linger. Not in sad realization of false friendship.

No, I grabbed that moment, squeezed it tight, and fired it right back off, carrying a spell that worked as well as any spell I've ever cast.

Maybe too well. I'd wanted to make sure I got the biggest, best deal offer anyone would get at that convention. I hadn't realized what I was sabotaging to get it.

I didn't just open a door with that spell. I flung it wide open. Slammed it hard enough to crack the drywall of reality – or at least this metaphor.

And I wouldn't realize what I'd done until Sunday night.

FOUR DAY CONVENTION. CHECK IN THURSDAY, PLUS EVENING PANELS. Then panels and meetings Friday through Sunday, and more events than any sane person would try to attend. To say nothing of an artist feeling overwhelming amounts of shyness in the aftermath of that phone message. It was all I could do to make myself attend panels, even the one I was on.

But I didn't have to go to people. They started coming to me, the moment my Thursday night panel finished.

Fanboys who wanted commissions. Local gallery owners who wanted showings. Three small publishers, all wanting me to free-lance book covers for them. And those weren't all.

By Friday night I already had more work than I could handle, and with each new offer I figured I'd run my spell out.

I wasn't even close.

By Saturday night video game companies wanted to set up meetings about licensing some of my fantasy art as the basis for games. That was way, way beyond anything I could have dreamt of for the convention. Jenny must have been getting tired of my excited phone calls about the latest great news.

It was Sunday afternoon when the big one dropped. SeaTac Productions, biggest and most up-and-coming film and television studio in the Pacific Northwest, wanted to contract me to do their high-end work. Mural-sized art for on-camera and for marketing.

That contract alone was more than enough to pay off my student loans. With enough left over to buy a house. Maybe even convince Jenny's parents that my art was a serious enough business to give me their blessing when I asked Jenny to marry me.

(Yeah, I could have used magic to open that door, but like I said, in almost all cases I don't use more magic than I have to. And I was pretty sure I could get their approval without magic. Well, *direct* magic, anyway.)

No doubt about it, I was riding higher than I ever had before. Almost drunk on the joy of how many things had gone right for me that weekend. So happy I'd all but forgotten about the one thing that had gone as far wrong as it could possibly have gone.

Until my elevator ride down to the Sheraton lobby.

The elevator was one of those big, mirrored affairs. The kind that couple probably hold a metric ton of geeks. And I was the only one in it, on my way back down from the SeaTac, so I smelled their citrus cleanser instead of *eau du conventioneer.*

I was hungry, and ready to splurge on steak and whatever passed for a microbrew north of the Colombia River.

I barely escaped the horde of incoming conventioneers, all heading for the third floor and some major ballroom event. I all but dove to the right as soon as the doors opened, before the zerg rush.

That was when I heard my name called.

"Hey! Jerry!"

I recognized the voice, and the moment I did it was as though the whole weekend hadn't happened. As though I hadn't had six-figures-plus of work thrown my way, and it was still afternoon with me listening to that damned voice mail message.

I tried to turn away, but I turned the wrong direction and found myself looking at Stu. Stu in a monkey suit, rumpled from too much wear this weekend, with the kind of hangdog look a bastard like him deserved for lying to me about his friendship all these years. Would have worked better if he still wore his brown hair long, but with that near-buzz but he couldn't quite pull it off.

The two of us stood there on the swirling browns of the marble tiles beside the elevators. Only the potted ficus trees next to us bearing witness to conversation that followed.

"You never called me back," he said. "What's up with that?"

"Sounded like you had a full load of meetings in your *suite.* Didn't want you to waste precious business meal time on some nobody you knew in college."

"Some nobody?" What looked like actual astonishment on his lying face. "Dude, you're the talk of the con."

"Yeah, how 'bout that?" My smile must have looked a little nasty, but I didn't mind. "Been pretty lucky, I guess."

"Lucky my ass," he said, almost sounding like his old encouraging self. "How many times have I told you your work's awesome?"

"Yeah," I said, "I'm probably keeping you from a meeting, so..."

"Naw, man," he said, his brown eyes almost haunted. "I was all set to conquer this convention like we talked about. Had maybe a dozen meetings lined up. But every one of them canceled. Even SeaTac Productions. I was sure I was going to get the bid for their marketing work. I even had a deal prepped that would have let me throw a bunch of work your way. Maybe even enough to cover your student loans. Get us both out of debt."

"Guess they decided to eliminate the middle-man."

Big words, but the truth was that something cold and heavy settled in my gut the moment Stu mentioned SeaTac Productions. Suddenly, dinner didn't sound so important.

"Yeah," Stu said. "Guess so." He shook his head and sighed. "I was going to propose to Allison, once I had this contract under my belt. Would have been enough money to raise a family, you know?"

"Shame," I said, and looking back I wonder if it was in response to what Stu said, or just me reciting how I felt.

Of course, that wasn't quite true. Yes, I felt ashamed that I'd snatched a deal right out from under Stu. And I had that big cold knot in my belly that I could tell was settling in for a long night.

But the truth is that I was still angry and hurt, and even through the shame I felt righteous. As though a liar like Stu didn't *deserve* such a good deal.

"That was why I got the suite," Stu said. "Figured I needed to look impressive. Success breeds success, right?"

"And ditching me was success?"

Anger. There was power in anger too. I felt it burning in my face.

Swimming in my head. I felt that anger even more than I felt that cold knot in my stomach. But I wasn't interested in power right then. I was more interested in laying into Stu over what he'd done.

"Leaving me with half the room fee we'd agreed to split? Skipping our whole plan of attack for the convention to do your own thing? Is that what successful guys do, Stu? Abandon their friends?"

Stu's face went ashen. "Jerry. I-I'm sorry. I didn't think—"

"Didn't think about old Jerry?" I poked his chest with my finger, and I honestly don't know where that came from. I was never a poke-people-in-the-chest kind of guy before that. "Or maybe didn't think I was really a friend anyway? Just a convenience."

"Convenience?" Stu's hands came up defensively, shoulders hunched at my tone. "No. Jerry. It wasn't like that. I was going to find time to—"

"You don't *find* time for the important people, Stu. You *make* time for the important people. And I'm through making time for you."

I stormed off then through a hail of Jerry-waits.

But I didn't go to dinner, or to any of the four end-of-con parties I'd been invited to. I went and hid in my room, while that cold knot of shame spread through my whole body. Set my ears ringing. My head reeling.

There's power in pain. But that power has a price.

The world has been a darker place since that convention. Fewer friends to call on, if they were ever really my friends. And while I have all those contracts and all that money coming in, the deadlines and the stress, they get to me too. Keep me up more nights than I'd like to admit.

And Jenny, I can't quite tell if she's giving me room or growing distant. That worries me.

Worst of all, each dark moment calls to me with its power. To use it. To make my world darker still.

I'm trying to find the power in laughter and joy again, but those moments keep slipping past. They feel fleeting. Only the dark moments try to linger.

And those dark moments. They're getting longer on their own.

COFFEE AND TREASON

Much as I love *James Bond* movies – I confess, I have yet to read any of the novels, though several are on my TBR* pile – I know full well that he's not a spy. He's an assassin.

Heck, even his designation, 007, represents that he has a license to kill.

Real espionage is about information. Gathering it. Controlling the flow of it. Disinformation campaigns. Spying and countering other spies.

It can be intense and thrilling in its own ways, though it doesn't lend itself to big action set pieces.

This story is about the kind of spy who might actually be working in Washington, D.C., right now. At least, the way I imagine he might be working.

As for *James Bond* style stories, I haven't written any yet. Though they itch at my mind from time to time...

*To Be Read

THE WIND OFF THE POTOMAC CARRIED THE STENCH OF DECAY. THAT more than anything else, told me it was spring.

Here in the Dee of Cee, spring is supposed to start in March. That's what everyone tells me. Me, though, I don't believe it. I'm not willing to call it spring until I can walk down the street first thing in the morning without an overcoat.

That's how it was for me, growing up around Detroit, and I still believed it here in the capital of the free world.

Holding onto beliefs was important in my line of work. Especially the big ones.

I couldn't afford to care who had the big chair. Which party was calling the legislative shots. Sure, I had my opinions, on a personal level, and I voted every election like a good citizen.

But when I was working, I had to believe in my country. That nebulous concept that said every man, woman and child in this big nation were all, ultimately on the same side.

Ours.

That was what made this kind of work so important. And so necessary. And so gut-wrenching, at times.

I was almost at the café when I saw that blue pickup drive past. Even in the busy morning traffic on Virginia Avenue, I could spot that two-year-old Ford F150. Wasted on these streets, with a driver who didn't haul anything more than his annual new big-screen television.

Good. Just on schedule.

I always had to worry about schedules when I was in disguise. Had to rely on public transit, so no one could make a vehicle like I just did. Had to move like someone who wasn't fit and in his thirties. Today, I had to look more than twice that old. Sure, that involved a few extra lines on the face, and a liberal sprinkling of gray through my short, usually black hair, but if I did the main things right, no one ever looked close enough to worry about my face.

I had on the oversize, gray pinstripe suit that was cut twenty years out of fashion, and the wide blue tie that went with it. Wrinkled, both the suit and the tie. They went with a hat in a style no one had worn in public since at least the Carter administration. Other pedestrians slid around me like speedboats around a tug.

My clothes didn't have to be oversize, but they helped hide my piece, and made me look like I'd lost weight with age. Shaky movements completed the image of a retiree with nothing but time on his hands. Not too much shaking. Just a little, but all the time. Modeled that after my gramps. He worked forty years on the lines for Ford, and when he retired he had this steady, low shaking in his hands and knees. Never seemed to stop, except when he slept.

And walking up the bustling sidewalk to that café, I moved in the perfect imitation of my gramps. Short, steady strides with just the right amount of shake.

Due to arrive at exactly ten-thirty-three, just like I had every Tuesday and Thursday for the last six weeks. All while gathering intel. The indoor-outdoor café was called The Shadow, a little joke on how close it was to The Mole. Should have been way too obvious a place for spies to meet.

But that's the way things ran in the Dee of Cee. Like a magic act. Everyone watched everyone, so most of what we did in the intelligence game, we did right up front where everyone could see it. No one cared if we knew who the Koreans were meeting with, or the Chinese, yadda yadda yadda.

But just like magicians, while we kept everyone looking at the stuff we wanted them to see, we were all sneaking around behind each other's backs.

And that was where the real magic happened.

I got to the café and was greeted by Shelly, my usual waitress. Shelly was a cute redhead, putting herself through Georgetown by working here, and actually using her job to meet as many staffers and lobbyists as she could, so she could get real internships in another year or two.

Smart girl. Probably didn't want me to put all that together over the weeks I'd been here, but gathering intel was second nature to me. Plus, playing the flirty old man was good cover. Made it look like I wasn't trying to avoid notice. Hiding in plain sight, and all that.

Also, that meant I got a better sense of the staff here at the Shadow. And I was pretty sure they were all just citizens, getting by.

I made sure to mention that in my reports.

Especially because this was the favored watering hole of Ivan Romanov, officially just a diplomatic aide so low down the totem pole he got cut out of everything important. The kind of guy who came across as just competent enough to hold down his position, a job gotten for him by an uncle who had an actual, important position as a diplomatic envoy to China.

All a lie, of course. Romanov was one of the more dangerous Russian agents here in the Dee of Cee. Lean, young, skilled, and every bit as patriotic as I was.

Six weeks ago I would have said he was just *an* agent, not the rest of it. But since I'd been coming here, all of my attention apparently on my cute waitress, I'd noticed him meeting with low-men on the totem pole from various other embassies.

And those weren't even spies. Well, not officially, anyway. They may not have ever realized that they were supplying vital information to a foreign government. From what I could tell, they honestly believed they were just ambitious men and women, frustrated in their lack of respect, meeting to commiserate with a fellow in the same quagmire.

Yeah, Romanov was that good.

So long as he was only meeting with reps from other countries, I didn't really care. I mean, my superiors cared, of course, so *professionally* I cared. My superiors wanted to know everything, and I passed on whatever I could pick up as I dined on my cinnamon roll and spiced, Jamaican coffee. Best coffee in the city, far as I was concerned.

No, my superiors may have cared about the details of what Romanov picked up from other embassies, but for me that was just part of the job.

I didn't care personally until the man with the blue pickup showed up last week.

Dan Smith. White House staffer, on the brink of execution.

Not literally, of course. But that was what we called it when anyone on an important staff was heading for a firing, and those were the ones we had to watch the closest. Because some of them got frustrated, and frustrated staffers all too often wanted to hurt someone.

That was what it usually came down to. Not the money, though they never said no. They always convinced themselves in their own heads that they were doing the right thing. Maybe some of them even thought they were whistleblowers.

But most of them had that set to the face, that crease to the brow and tightness to the lips.

Anger. Frustration. The need to lash out and hurt someone.

Then they'd do something they'd regret for the rest of their lives.

According to his record, Dan Smith wasn't that kind of guy. All his psych profiles pegged him as happy-go-lucky. The kind of guy who'd fall out of one position and land at a better one.

And, in fact, that was what he was set up for. He'd already figured out that the axe was coming, and from what I read in his profile, he had a job lined up with a lobbying firm. One that paid him almost half again what he made at the House, plus more vacation time. Not the kind of guy who turned informant to foreign governments.

Could have called it pure luck that I spotted him here, meeting with Romanov. But nothing in this business is pure luck.

I was here because one of my bosses had a gut feeling about Romanov. A gut feeling I'd confirmed in spades.

And I was the kind of guy to show up an hour before he was supposed to, and leave an hour late. At least, whenever it wouldn't draw attention. I'd made the habit of sitting on the bench across the street from The Shadow before my waitress came on shift, then coming in after she'd been there a good half-hour or so. Long enough to settle in. Then, after I ate – and took my time about it – I'd head back to my bench to slowly sip my refill, and anyone watching would think I was daydreaming about my pretty, redheaded waitress.

Just another dirty old man, in a city full of dirty old men.

That was how I'd spotted Danny boy. He'd shown outside the time frame of Romanov's meet-ups. Been there waiting for him last week. Said he'd have something big for him, if he was interested.

And today it was supposed to go down.

I love my country. And I love its citizens. So, to me, there is nothing lower in this world than someone who'd knowingly give aid and comfort to the enemy.

That was why I didn't care about most of Romanov's meetings. They weren't with *our* people. They weren't even with people trying to do something wrong. They were just another case of a good spy doing his job. If I got mad about that, I'd be a hypocrite.

But Danny boy, he went out of his way to meet someone from the Russian embassy and offer state secrets. And they had to be state secrets, the way old Romanov's eyes lit up when Danny whispered in his ear last week.

I didn't catch the amount of the offer. Wish I had. Not personally. Personally, I didn't care if he was being offered the goose that laid the golden eggs. No amount of money is worth treason. No, I only wish I'd caught the amount because I hate turning in an incomplete report.

I arrived right on schedule that morning, well before Dan Smith found his parking space.

Shelly met me with a smile, whisked me quickly to my favorite table, right in the corner, just inside the little wrought iron fence, and up against the brown siding of the café itself. Put me under the awning, safe from weather and sun. Gave me the perfect view of Shelly's station there by the entrance to the building itself. And more important, gave me an "incidental" view of Romanov's table.

Helped that it was still only just spring. Sane people, ordinary citizens, didn't want to eat outside in the chill morning air, with that stench coming in off the Potomac. Almost all the tables out here were empty. Just Romanov, me, and these four college kids who took the center table every Tuesday to pontificate at each other about politics and philosophy.

And they had to be loud, to hear each other over the traffic. If it hadn't been for my "hearing aid" I'd never have been able to listen in on Romanov's conversations.

All the tables and chairs out here on the cobblestones were wrought iron, as much as a check against the weather as an attempt at a restaurant style. Napkin holders in the table centers, next to little bowls of packets for salt, sugar, pepper and creamer.

Romanov sat in the opposite corner from me, his back against the siding. He drank his coffee black. A strong, Russian blend. Never ate anything, just smoked his foul cigarettes and drank his strong coffee.

Might have been a defense against the odor of the Potomac. Or maybe he was stuck in the Eighties. Nothing about either in his file.

"Here's your roll and coffee, Emilio," Shelly said to me with a broad smile, using my cover name, of course. "Love the carnation, by the way. You meeting with a girl later?"

I stammered out an answer through a forced blush. Something off the cuff about a woman named Agnes, clearly made up by an old man who didn't want to look like he was trying to impress a young girl.

Inside, I was squirming. She'd noticed the carnation in my hat. I'd hoped it suited the look enough to not draw attention. If she'd noticed it, Romanov might notice it. Might suspect something. Might even guess it contained the camera that would let me catch his deal with Dan on film.

Sloppy. But I knew better than to sit there, calling myself an idiot inside my head and wishing I'd thought to have a flower in my hat every day like I should have.

No, I stuffed cinnamon roll into my mouth and chewed. Barely letting myself notice the wonderful taste and the way the cinnamon highlighted the drizzle. I was too busy letting my eyes roam anywhere but Shelly in my apparent embarrassment, fighting hard to hold that blush a little longer.

Let me spot Dan coming in, quick on his feet in a black suit and tie as though he were in ... mourning...

That was the missing piece. Someone died. Someone important. And Dan was in mourning. Not in his file, so it couldn't have been a relative or a Dee of Cee known associate, but I was sure I was right.

This wasn't about money, this was personal for Dan. That made it even more potentially dangerous.

And worse than that, Dan wasn't alone.

Oh, he walked in alone, on quick steps as though he was in a hurry. His expression the usual New-Yorker-down-for-a-visit kind of harried, as though the whole city moved too slow for him.

But a dozen paces behind him, a big bruiser of a bald white man. The kind with tattoos just hidden by his suit shirt, and his suit tailored to look too small so he looked even more impressive.

I didn't buy it. He moved too well in the suit. It may have looked too tight, but I had no doubt he could fight in it. I also had no doubt he had a piece under his left armpit.

And the bruiser was watching Dan and Romanov at the same time. Might even have noticed me, if I hadn't just let my gaze wander toward Shelly with a not-quite-suppressed sigh.

Romanov was staring at the bruiser. Dan stood at the table, hand in the inside pocket of his suit. Rookie mistake. Half the people watching would have thought he had his hand on a gun. Lucky for him the college kids didn't care, and Shelly was inside at the moment.

I knew he didn't have a weapon. Dan had never even been to a pistol range, much less purchased a weapon.

No, he had his hand on whatever he was selling.

But Romanov wasn't looking at Dan. He was looking at the bruiser.

Finally, without looking away from the bruiser, who was now staring back at Romanov in open threat, Romanov pointed to an empty chair at his table.

Dan leaned in. Said something harsh and quiet that I couldn't quite pick out over wind and traffic noise, not to mention the clinking of dishes from inside the open door into the café proper.

Romanov pointedly sipped his coffee, still staring at the bruiser.

Dan wasn't having it. Started to turn away.

Romanov tripped him. Subtle move, shifted a chair across the cobblestones just enough to catch Dan's foot. Wouldn't have seen it happen if I hadn't been sitting in the right place, so no way the bruiser saw it go down.

But we all saw Dan go down. Fell forward with his arms waving. Landed jaw-first on a cobblestone, while something fell out of his suit jacket. Went the opposite way from a dislodged tooth.

A flash drive.

It bounced on the cobblestones into the center of the outside portion of the café. Near the table of the four college kids.

Romanov stood.

The bruiser came rushing in, hand inside his jacket.

Romanov's hand went into his jacket.

The bruiser stopped moving. Just inside the gate.

They stared at each other. Twenty feet apart. Each with a hand on the grip of a pistol.

The college kids were too deep in their discussion to notice.

Meanwhile, Dan was on the ground. Dazed, but not quite out. Shelly came running over to him. Helped him sit up.

"Oh, my," I said in my quavery voice as I stood. "You poor young man."

I made my shaky way closer. My expression all concern. My vision centered on Shelly and Dan, but my peripheral vision entirely watching Romanov.

Romanov looked at me.

His hand left his jacket.

Made me. In that moment I was sure of it. Must have seen something off in my makeup. Maybe my posture. Maybe just the kind of instinct that lets people like us survive in our business.

Damn.

Romanov pulled his hand out of his jacket, straightened up, dusted off his jacket, and strode out of the café. The bruiser turned with him, hand still inside his jacket, but made no move to stop him.

Shelly had Dan in a wrought iron chair now, and the college kids had finally realized something was wrong. They were all up, and rushing around, and arguing about ice or napkins and I think some kind of homeopathic crap.

I didn't care.

"I believe I saw your tooth," I said, dropping to all fours and going straight for the flash drive.

Dan was still dazed. Maybe didn't notice the flash drive.

The bruiser did.

"Tooth's over there," he said, pointing, his voice deep and menacing as his look.

"No, no," I said, "I'm sure it's this way."

The bruiser dropped and hustled to that flash drive before I could get to it. At least, without ditching my disguise, and I wasn't willing to go that far. Maybe Romanov made me, or maybe the scene was just too hot and he wanted to clear out.

For all I knew, he was across the street right now, keeping an eye on what we were doing.

I had to stay in character a little longer yet.

The bruiser knocked aside a chair and a college kid and grabbed the flash drive. Stood up.

Shelly grabbed Dan's tooth. Turned on her knees to offer it to him.

Dan saw what the bruiser was holding. His eyes got wide. He jumped to his feet. Started moving, the bruiser falling into step beside him.

"Your tooth," Shelly said, holding it up, her expression all amazement.

"Kee' i'" Dan said, napkin to his mouth and hustling even faster as he reclaimed the flash drive and shoved it back in his pocket.

I grimaced. Shook my head.

I sent the text message that would have agents converge on Dan the moment he got back to his car.

I sighed, disgusted. Made my quavery way back to my seat to finish my breakfast.

Yeah, I'd stopped the sale. Yeah, Dan would get arrested. But it wasn't enough. We could get him for possession of state secrets, maybe even with intent to sell. But without the amount, and without pictures of the sale, we couldn't nail him for treason. Couldn't officially nail Romanov either.

Still, as I finished off my cinnamon roll, I tried to console myself. I'd made my country just a little bit safer today.

***

Turned out to be a bigger deal than it felt at the time.

Dan Smith had lost his childhood friend Stevie Rickenbacker. A reporter, overseas, dead because of friendly fire during one of the lesser known conflicts in the Middle East. Dan had been mad enough to get his hands on deployment and movement intel, and the bastard was going to sell it to the Russians with an eye to getting it to somebody even worse.

Apparently the fact that it had been a friendly fire accident was enough to make Dan lash out at his own country's troops.

So much for happy-go-lucky. Got him a nice bit of time at a very bad place.

And the intel I'd gathered on Romanov was enough to get him officially kicked out of the country. Ostensibly it had been as a favor to China, over something Romanov had found out, but at least he wasn't here anymore.

Of course, he was still at large, and still dangerous.

And worse, he did make me. So my old man disguise was dead, and my ability to work the Dee of Cee was severely compromised.

Got me a year of desk duty, but the director himself promised he'd try to get me an overseas assignment when the year was up.

Maybe someplace warm. With good coffee.

FROZEN

No, this has nothing to do with Disney, or singing snowmen, or anything like that.

This is one of my time stories. Not time travel in this case, but about a man who finds himself stuck between moments in time. Unsure of how he can get back into the flow of time again.

The answer, of course, isn't what he expects.

As a point of potential interest here, I've actually taken exactly the drive that the main character takes in this story. Same basic freeway, same basic car, very similar situation.

If I got frozen outside of time, though, I don't remember it. Then again, would I?

THERE ARE MOMENTS IN LIFE WHEN YOU WISH TIME WOULD STOP, AND moments when it actually does. The former are usually the best moments. Love and friendship and fun. But the latter, well, it only happened to me once.

Too late at night for the speed I was driving. Especially in the rain. But I was eighteen and convinced of my immortality, like we all were at that age. Considering I had to be up at six a.m. to open Dream On Records – the last actual record store in Santa Josita, California, just another Bay Area suburb – I had no business staying at that party until two. But I did.

What can I tell you? Trina Dalman was talking to me. *Me.* As in, the party was going on inside Pierre's parents' place, and it was just the Blonde Goddess Herself and *me* on the patio. Both of us finding excuses to keep the other talking until we made an honest-to-God date for Saturday night.

Yeah, it was a stupid date – mini-golf and pizza – but it was going to be just the two of us, and she'd already hinted that she loved the view from that rest area up Skyline Drive. And I knew what view *I* wanted to see on Skyline Drive.

So, yeah, maybe I'd been awake some twenty hours, but I was so bouncy excited about my date that I was sure I could have run all the way home if I had to. Even in the rain. Driving seemed like nothing.

I had Three Coyotes cranked up on the stereo of The Fossil, which was what I called my 1992 Pontiac Sunfire, and was blazing my way up 280N from San Jose. 280N was everything a freeway ought to be – wide and smooth, with lots of lanes, and rises and dips, and enough curves to keep me thinking of Trina. I still had the taste of light beer in my mouth, but I hadn't had a drop in over an hour to make sure I was safe to drive.

Usually, driving 280 at that hour meant that most of the lights I'd see were on the side of the freeway along the hills, so green in the wintertime. Most nights, the view in my rearview mirror would be black as outer space, and up ahead I'd be lucky to see one or two cars over the whole thirty-mile stretch from Pierre's parents' place.

Most nights. But not that night.

The freeway wasn't exactly *packed*, but it felt that way because I was in a hurry. Cars were scattered everywhere, and they all seemed to be doing that I'm-not-drunk thing. That thing where they'd weave just a little in their lanes, and drive about three miles off the actual speed limit, either a little high or a little low or varying between the two.

It was as though everyone was having their Christmas party two weeks early, all on the same rainy night, and the partygoers had dipped into the eggnog a little heavy before driving home.

And I did not have time for speed limit driving. So I just pretended the cars were asteroids and wove between and around them at high speed, laughing and whooping and still high-fiving myself about having a date with *Trina Dalman.*

I was just turning back to face front after leveling a Monty Python insult at some idiot. Honestly. Driving his red Lexus Coupe under the speed limit in the fast lane. He hit his horn at me. I hit mine at him. Some other people were hitting theirs, but I couldn't see who.

Then I got my eyes forward again, and I saw the worst sight this side of hell.

Brake lights. Everywhere.

All four lanes ahead of me were full, and they were all stopped. Some of them must have been adding to the horn symphony.

They'd been hidden by a curve and an incline, and my looking behind me hadn't helped. Exhausted and giddy as I was, even if I'd been going the speed limit on dry ground, I might have been hard-pressed to stop in time. As it was...

Crash. Incoming. Maybe three seconds.

Three.

I slammed on the brakes. They locked. My tires screamed for mercy on the wet pavement.

Two.

I tried whipping the wheel away. Tried to aim for the guardrail. Steering wheel locked. I was bound straight for the rear bumper of a great big SUV, complete with Baby On Board bumper sticker, and tons of camping gear strapped to the roof.

One.

I yanked my emergency brake and closed my eyes.

I STOPPED?

That was my first thought when I opened my eyes. It didn't make sense, but I actually thought for a moment that I managed to halt my speeding car.

I actually got as far as whooping before pieces of the scene around me started clicking in my head, and they didn't add up to a coherent puzzle.

First, my car wasn't scant inches from the bumper of that SUV. I had to be a good twenty feet back, which was just about exactly how far back I'd been when I yanked the emergency brake.

Second, it was quiet. Like dead-of-night-in-a-closet-hiding-from-your-brother quiet. No more honking horns. No squeal of my brakes. No drumming of the rain. Even my music stopped.

Third, and that this was third and not first tells you something about my state of mind, I was just sitting comfortably in my seat. No deploying airbags trying to protect me from my sudden stop. No chest pain from getting thrown against the seat belt.

Those were all things that came and went through my mind in short order, dizzying in their nonsensicalness. What cemented for me that something was wrong was what I saw next.

The Lexus Coupe. In my rear view mirror.

Frozen.

I might not have been in the best state of mind, but I'd been guessing that the Lexus driver had been tippling from the eggnog a little more than most of my fellow drivers because I just couldn't imagine why else he would have been driving under the speed limit in the fast lane of a freeway built for speed at freaking two-fifteen in the morning.

Then I saw his face. Moments before, he'd been business-man

arrogant, with his Clark Kent haircut and his judgmental eyebrows as he'd pounded the horn at me.

Now, his face was frozen in a scream.

Frozen.

That was when I realized the rain had stopped mid-downpour. And I don't mean the rain went away. I mean I could see hundreds of droplets hanging in the air, halted on their way to the ground.

That made all the pieces slam together in my head. Jingly cold jolted through my system. I screamed, and it came out louder than ever in all that silence.

I lost a minute or two, just manic. I beat on the horn – which didn't blare – I yanked on the emergency brake – which was already high as it would go. I saw that my speedometer still read fifty miles per hour and panic just ripped right through me.

I had to get out. I was going to crash and I had to get out.

I popped the seat belt, threw open my door and dove onto the asphalt.

I rolled to a halt against stiff green grass, that didn't particularly want to yield just because I was bumping up against it. I felt the bumps, but none of it hurt. I expected at least a scuffed elbow or a bruised thigh, but when I stopped rolling, I felt fine. A little wet from diving through raindrops and rolling on wet ground, but otherwise normal.

I got up. Patted myself off as I looked around. No one else was moving. Everyone else seemed to be frozen in that single instance. I could see two little toe-headed kids in the SUV looking back at my car as though it never occurred to them that it might hit them.

The idiot in the Lexus still staring straight forward, mid-scream. No sign that he'd seen me dive out of my car.

My car door was still open though. That was something. Some small sign of change in this weird fever dream.

What was the last thing I did? The last thing before everything froze?

I yanked on my e-brake. And I prayed. Did I pray? I assume I must have. No atheists in foxholes and all that jazz.

Was that what this was? Was some god, some guardian angel maybe, stopping the world in answer to my prayer?

"Hello?" I called. "Anybody?"

I tried to remember the name of that angel from *It's a Wonderful Life*, but it just wouldn't come. Couldn't have been the same angel anyway. That guy got his wings at the end of the movie.

Didn't matter. Nobody answered me anyway, even though I called a few more times.

By now the shock was wearing off and curiosity set in. Just what was happening and why? Maybe I'd had an accident, and I was in a coma. Making this some sort of coma fantasy. Or maybe a half-conscious fugue state where I was trying to piece my life back together, but when I woke up I'd have amnesia or something.

Seemed pretty coherent for a fugue state though. Detailed too. No two of the raindrops were quite identical. And I could get up close and personal to look. They were slightly different lengths and thicknesses.

I ... I don't know why I lost time trying to find a pattern in the raindrops. I think maybe I'd convinced myself that there was some kind of secret hidden among them. That whatever was going on was, in fact, a divine act. Even if no choirs of angels showed up to sing answers to me in three-part harmony.

No way to know how much time I wasted that way. Wasn't as though the clock on my phone was changing. It was stuck at two-fifteen and fifty-eight seconds.

The other reason it was hard to gauge how long I wasted that way, was that I wasn't changing either. I mean, my heart wasn't pounding the way it was when I grabbed the e-brake, but I still had that jittery adrenaline I'm-going-to-die sense all through my body. Still had that cold fear too, even if it didn't really demand my attention anymore.

All right. I've got to be honest with you, even though this is the freakiest part for me to even think about.

I'm pretty sure my heart wasn't beating.

I was moving around, and I must have been breathing because I sure had enough air to let me scream and yell. But when I realized I still felt that adrenaline rush, I tried to take my pulse.

Nothing.

Not at either wrist. Not at my neck. I even pressed my fingertips to my chest in three places, trying to find a heartbeat. And I found nothing.

That was enough to send another jolt of fear through me, but the adrenaline and jitters didn't get any worse.

I knew it then. I had to be dead.

DECIDING I WAS DEAD ACTUALLY SENT A WAVE OF PEACE THROUGH ME. Didn't stop the jitters or the bounciness, even if I felt a little sad that I wouldn't live to go on that date with Trina. But still, dead, right? As in, all my cares were gone now and I got to find out what happened next.

Except that if this was next, nothing was happening.

"So," I called out to the rain-cloud-filled heavens above. "What happens now? Does the grim reaper come to collect me? An angel, maybe? A Valkyrie?

"Is anyone even listening?"

No answer.

Well, I was not going to stand here not getting any older while some cosmic bureaucratic snafu kept me in limbo.

I started checking out the other cars. I figured maybe, just maybe, there was someone else dead like me, and sitting in their car. Maybe just as puzzled as I was. Or maybe even more puzzled, if they hadn't figured out the dead part yet.

I made sure not to look back at my car as I started into the crowd of traffic ahead of me. One, I figured my dead body might be sitting behind the wheel, and who needed to see that? And two, if the car door was open, then that might indicate I was still corporeal, and thus not actually dead. And I was starting to groove a bit on the notion of being dead, so if I was wrong, I didn't want to harsh my buzz just yet.

Typical Bay Area mix of cars, by which I mean everything from old heaps held together by rust and prayers all the way up to six-figure beasts by Ferrari and Tesla, with the ages and nationalities of their passengers as diverse as the makes and models of cars.

The only consistent thing? They were all frozen.

I must have checked some fifty cars on my way to the front of this mess, and in every single one, every single passenger was frozen. Even the babies and animals, 'cause I wasn't discounting any possibilities here.

But nope. I was the only one up and about, all the way up to the front of the line. Up at the front, a few of the drivers were getting out of their cars, but they were frozen mid-attempt.

Two car wreck causing all this traffic, blocking four lanes. One of the cars was an old tank of a station wagon that someone had managed to keep running since the 1970s. The other was a late model SUV, the kind with all the bells and whistles.

The right front bumper on the station wagon was ripped clean off. The rear left bumper of the SUV was wrecked hard enough to snap the axle, if the angle of the wheel was any indication.

The station wagon had the kind of family my dad would call trailer park trash, whether or not they lived in a trailer park. Pasty white and overweight, all six of them. But they'd all had their seatbelts on and looked no worse for wear.

The SUV had a Japanese American family, five of them. They looked fine too. Airbags all deployed. Didn't see any blood or pained expressions. Panicked and worried expressions aplenty, but nobody who looked hurt.

The dads of both families had been driving, but they were out of their cars and looked to have been frozen mid-yelling match in the middle of the freeway.

Farther down the freeway I could see two highway patrol cars coming, driving the wrong way down the empty section of freeway. Well, they'd been driving when time stopped, anyway. In that instant, they might as well have been ten miles away.

Everything looked under control. Bad, sure, but nothing fatal. Nothing that seemed to me to be worth stopping time on this end.

That was when I saw the doll.

It was a little Wonder Woman doll, sitting in the middle of the fast lane, maybe two dozen feet from the SUV. My eyes tracked from the doll to the SUV, where a little girl in the backseat was staring out the half-open car window at the doll.

She already had one hand going for the door latch.

I looked back up the freeway at the inbound patrol cars. The drivers' eyes were fixed on the mid-freeway confrontation.

They might not even see one little girl toddling onto the asphalt for a doll.

And what about the front line of the impatient cars behind me? What if one of those drivers tried to go around?

Seemed like the most obvious thing in the world for me to pick up the doll and put it in the hand of the little girl reaching for the door latch.

I have to admit. When I did, I half-expected that this was the magic key. That I was here, in a moment of frozen rainstorm on a freeway, to save a little girl's life. That maybe, when I put the doll back in her hand, I'd find myself back behind the wheel of The Fossil that magically managed to avoid an accident because I'd done the Right Thing (trademark pending).

That wasn't how it worked.

When I finished ranting my disappointment at my continued imprisonment between seconds, I wandered back toward my car.

I confess. I did consider just walking away somewhere. Home, maybe, or back to see Trina even if she couldn't see me. And I'd like to say that the reason I didn't was that it would have felt ghostly, that I would have felt alone and cut off from the world. All that teenage angst crap.

Honestly, though, it just felt too darn far to walk. Maybe I wouldn't get any more tired than I already was, but I really didn't have any way to know that. I just knew when I thought about the distances involved, all I really wanted to do was go back to my car and await the inevitable. Whatever it turned out to be.

Personally, I was hoping the inevitable brought a breakfast burrito.

But when I got back to my car – door open and no dead me inside – I didn't climb back inside.

Instead, I looked at the angle. I mean, the car was still going about fifty, though the emergency brake would have something to say about that, and my efforts at spinning the steering wheel hadn't done enough to clear the bumper of that huge, camping-gear-laden SUV. An SUV with two families inside and about ten people altogether.

From the way I judged the angle, my car was bound to hit that bumper. Maybe to the left side instead of dead on, but I was still pretty sure "dead" would end up being the key word before all the smoke cleared.

So I climbed up on top of the SUV and started looking through the camping gear. Handing the doll to the little girl had made me think – no matter what happened to me, time had to start again eventually, and there had to be some way to get my car to miss that SUV.

I found a good, solid wooden oar. I jammed that oar under the front right tire of my car just as hard as I could. Didn't get far, but it would be enough for some traction.

I had to hunt among the hills at the side of the road to find a big enough rock to do the job I had in mind. It also had to be one I could carry, but past a certain point, size was only going to do so much good anyway.

I got the rock under the oar at what I hoped was the right spot.

That was when time started again.

THE REST SHOWED UP IN THE ACCIDENT REPORT. MY CAR WAS SPEEDING right for that rock, when the oar fell in my path. Wedged my car on two wheels, where it flipped onto the shoulder. Missed the SUV by maybe six inches.

Luckiest guy in the world that I was that day, I got thrown clear before The Fossil rolled. Paramedics found me on the side of the road, half-conscious but generally unharmed. Mostly in shock, they said.

The Fossil was totaled, but I was still able to keep my date with Trina the next night. And I had one heck of a story to tell her.

IF YOU KILL HITLER....

Now here's a time travel story. Maybe.

Obviously, the idea of killing Hitler is heavily enmeshed in the idea of time travel. Would you? Could you? Should you?

This story approaches that question from a very different angle, while telling a very different story. That's about all I really feel I can say about it, without spoiling something. So I'll stop here.

WILLIE DIDN'T FIGURE TIME TRAVEL WOULD CHANGE ANYTHING.

Sure, he heard about the discovery on the news, same as everyone else. Thing was, he figured it didn't apply to him. Discovery that big, no doubt the government was going to conscript and redact and twist and pontificate, until the only people who ever got to make use of the discovery were the sort who signed their lives away to government service.

Willie wasn't a big believer in government "service." Not since he got out. Volunteering, that was service he could get behind. Food kitchens every Saturday. Playing guitar for people on hospice every Tuesday and Thursday afternoon. That was service. That was making a difference in people's lives.

The government stuff, he'd seen enough of in his two-year stint as a grunt. Living under threat in bad conditions to shoot bullets at people over ... some political disagreement or other.

Six countries in twenty-four months. Must have fired off more rounds than he earned dollars during that time. And it was during those two years that Willie did something that, well, no amount of volunteer service could ever make up for.

So, yeah, maybe time travel didn't apply to guys like Willie.

Still.

When he heard about time travel on the noisy television up over the counter at the Gravy Caboose – his personal favorite greasy spoon because of how well they made chicken waffles with gravy fries – he had a fleeting thought that maybe, just maybe, he could go back in time himself.

Be Private Willie McTavish one more time, to set right what he did that day...

THE JUNGLE MAY NOT HAVE BEEN HOTTER THAN THE DESERT WAS, BUT here the heat clung as bad as the stinky mud. Heat so damp it was like Willie woke up sweating. Like his shorts never made it into the dryer, but he had to wear them anyway, and his fatigues were even worse.

And "fatigues" was right. Damp as they were, they must have weighed ten pounds more than normal. Not something he noticed first thing in the morning, but after that afternoon march, then the firefight with the "rebels" – harsh term for people fighting for their own way of life, which Willie considered none of his business – just wearing them was exhausting. His clothes felt like lead and his pack so heavy he might have been carrying his whole platoon.

Maybe not the *whole* platoon. Maybe just the ones who'd died in the firefight. Hicks, Brayburn, Collins, and Devereaux.

Only eight guys in Willie's squad still among the living when they found that burned out village. And it was a village, not a town or a city. Willie's squad been briefed on this. There were still small tribes in Africa. Nomads mostly. Not part of any one nation, but allowed to go their own way as long as they stuck to certain restricted areas, because the muckety-mucks had decreed it. And because Uncle Sam gave the affected nations money.

There were reasons. Willie didn't care.

All he cared about right then was a place to drop for a little while. Close his eyes. Let his heart rate get back to something like normal. Maybe get the chance to unclench his shoulders and jaw. Take a minute to think about the dead. Maybe say a prayer.

The village wasn't much. Grass and wicker huts over a dry dirt clearing. Mostly burned away, but a few walls left to give something like shelter. More important was the dry dirt. "Dry" was like a half-remembered dream.

The sergeant didn't want to stop. Said the villages were keep-away zones for us G.I. Joes. The ell tee overruled him. Said it was burnt out by the locals to drive the tribe away before the fighting came close. Said other things too, but by the time he got to them, the rest of the squad was horizontal and it didn't much matter.

Mattered to Sarge.

Willie'd been the first one to drop his pack on the lovely dry ground, so Willie was the first of two named to perimeter guard. Not enough of the squad left for a proper perimeter, and they all needed rest something fearsome, so Willie got one one-eighty and Johnson got the other.

Getting back up was Hell. Holding his rifle again was worse. But worst of all, he had the one-eighty facing the jungle. Ferns and trees and flowers in wild colors. That damp, decay smell like it was all dying right in front of him, the way Devereaux had.

Every inch of it could have hidden guys who wanted nothing more than to shoot Willie. Or at least who were willing to pull the trigger at Willie for traveling thousands of miles and trying to tell them they were on the wrong side.

Willie's arms were shaking, holding the rifle. His eyes teared up. So very tired, but his heart was pounding like it was trying to outrun stampeding elephants. Every crack and snap jerked his head, every strange bird cry raised his rifle.

Willie was going to die here. He was sure of it.

Then it happened. A face popped into view. And there was a rifle. Willie was sure he saw a rifle. Absolutely positive in the moment that just under that ink-dark face, a rifle came up like it was going to point at him in the next second or two.

Willie stopped breathing. Couldn't hear anything but the rush of his own blood.

This was it. Him or this "rebel." This poor soul who had nothing against Willie except that Willie was where he was, doing what he was doing. This poor bastard who had more right to shoot Willie than Willie had to shoot him.

But the instinct to survive was a powerful, powerful thing.

Willie only had maybe a second. But in that time his rifle sprang into firing position.

A burst of automatic weapon fire made the air stink of gunpowder. Made the rifle even hotter in Willie's blistered and clenching hands.

Maybe the same moment. Maybe just after. Willie wasn't sure, exactly. But the rest of the squad, they started shooting too.

Tore up that little patch of jungle something fierce.

Turned out, wasn't rebels, and they weren't armed. Villagers, where they weren't supposed to be. Hiding from the war, instead of moving on to someplace safe.

No cameras and no witnesses. Didn't matter. Willie confessed the whole thing right to the colonel when they got back to the base. Spent days waiting for the M.P.s. The tribunal.

Wasn't 'til later he found out, the ell tee and the colonel were old family friends. That the colonel buried the incident – and Willie's report – the way the squad buried the bodies.

Deep.

* * *

JUST ABOUT NINETY DAYS AFTER THE WORST DAY IN WILLIE'S LIFE, HE was discharged. Word was, the whole squad was, minus the ell tee, and Sarge. Honorable, according to the forms.

After Willie'd filled out those forms, two guys in black suits had come in and made very, very clear to Willie that he was never to talk about that day, or he'd spend the rest of his life in a rubber room.

Just about three years after the worst day in Willie's life, he still woke up sweating. Still wondered what the hell he'd thought was a rifle. Branch, maybe?

And it was that incident that Willie thought of as he sat at the counter of the Gravy Caboose and watching the news segment about time travel.

Willie daydreamed about going back in time. Stopping himself from shooting, maybe. Or maybe just getting those villagers to flee to safety. He liked the latter idea better. Figured it had a better chance of making sure those poor villagers stayed safe.

Didn't matter though, and Willie knew it. Time travel, that was for the muckety-mucks. Or maybe for the rich, and Willie was a lot of things, but rich wasn't one of them.

So Willie tried not to get his hopes up. Tried to ignore the follow-up stories and in-depth articles and exposés and all the other segments about time travel over the coming months.

Wasn't easy. Even the sports section talked about how time travel might affect records we've always thought of as set in stone. DiMaggio's hitting streak. Cy Young's wins. Settle questions like who knew what about the Black Sox scandal, and whether or not Rose gambled on the sport.

Just when things reached the point that Willie was ready to give up on the news altogether, the time travel stories just stopped. Maybe they actually faded away like most news stories do, but to Willie it seemed as though one day the stories were freaking everywhere, and the next the news was back to murders and politics. Business as usual.

Guy, at the counter of the Gravy Caboose, tried to make some kind of conspiracy theory about it. Got his voice all hush-hush and went on about how the government had the real thing and they were keeping it quiet and such like.

Willie didn't see the point of the hush-hush tones. Figured it never could have been any other way. If there was time travel, of course the government controlled it.

And Willie continued to think that. Right up to the grand opening of Time of Your Life, the first time travel center in the Bay Area. Mountain View, to be exact. Dead center of Silicon Valley, of course, which made it not much more than twenty miles from Willie's apartment down in Gilroy.

Willie tried to ignore it. Wasn't easy, because the news did "features" and spot segments, not to mention the place did a metric ton of advertising. But Willie figured it was for the rich people. The Silicon Valley billionaires, or the venture capitalists, or just the old money Atherton types.

But then the dream came back.

Every night, Willie was back in that village. Every night he was pulling the trigger. But it wasn't just the covering jungle he saw getting blown apart. Wasn't just the smell of gunpowder and the chatter of his rifle. No. In the dream, he saw every face. Heard every scream. Smelled their blood and their perforated bowels.

And every time, Willie woke up screaming and sweating.

Willie survived three months of that before he couldn't take it anymore. If it took every dollar he had, if it took the rest of his life to pay it off, Willie had to go back. He had to make things right.

He had to.

THE TIME OF YOUR LIFE PARKING LOT WASN'T SMALL – THE PLACE looked like a converted grocery store, complete with plenty of parking – but it was *jammed*. Willie rumbled around for about ten minutes in his beat-up old Chevy S-10 pickup before he gave up and found street parking about two blocks away.

Willie'd been hoping that a Saturday morning in the spring would have been empty at a place like that. Hoped his breakfast shift at the shelter let him out early enough to beat the crowds.

Apparently he was wrong.

The inside of the place was done in blue and purple swirls of tile, and it had colorful posters of different times and places. Victorian parties. Gladiator fights in ancient Rome. The deck of the Titanic. The battle of Bannockburn. Woodstock and about a dozen other concert posters. The coronations of Queen Elizabeth II, Henry V, and others. More posters and times than Willie could begin to count.

One prominent poster, bigger than the others, showed a black and white photo of Hitler in his Nazi uniform, with huge yellow letters that read: "Kill Hitler!"

Willie did wonder how much they could charge for that, given that it could only be done once.

The cross-section of people all sitting around the huge lobby and filling out forms was amazing. Young and old, some in the latest fashions, others with clothes almost falling apart. Seemed that not only did everyone *want* to travel through time, but maybe, just maybe, everyone could *afford* it. Maybe not the Hitler package, but the chance to fix some misstep in life, to right some small wrong.

Or maybe, like Willie, some of them had a really, really big wrong to set right.

The harried lady at the counter shoved a clipboard with a form at Willie, gave him a number tag – Willie's number was three eighty-six – and turned away to the next customer.

Willie found a seat off near the front window, next to a ficus, at the end of a row that held one big family. They all had pleasant features, well-groomed hair and clothes, and spoke in excited, hushed tones about meeting someone named Smith.

The form didn't take Willie long. Mostly health questions and disclaimers. Willie'd filled out hundreds of forms like that in the service. Sure, on this one he had to lie in a couple of places, but that was par for the course. Truth was, Willie didn't care if he came back broken, crazy or dead. Not so long as he saved those villagers.

Waiting for his number, that took a little longer. But waiting was another skill honed to a fine edge in the service. Rush, rush, rush, then sit on your hands for hours on end before it's rush, rush, rush again.

Willie didn't miss that.

Finally, though, Willie's number was called.

It wasn't an office, so much as a cubicle among a good dozen. That same gray cloth for the walls that Willie saw every time a delivery took him past the front desk of one company or another. This one smelled like aerosol potpourri.

In the cubicle, just a man with a keyboard, sitting in a leather executive chair. He wore a black suit – jacket draped over the back of the chair – but a vivid purple tie over his crisp, white shirt. His haircut was just as crisp. Sarge would've approved. He wore big glasses, the kind that had a computer HUD where he could see it and Willie couldn't.

"Sit down, sit down," the man said with a smile full of bright teeth. He kept talking before Willie could even sit in the red, rolling visitor's chair. "You look like the ex-military type. Let me guess."

He looked Willie up and down. Pointed his finger at him. "You want to kill Hitler?"

"No, I, uh—"

"Because if you kill Hitler, be sure to get the tee shirt on this visit. We don't keep records of where you went or what you did, so after you leave there'll be no way to prove you qualify for the shirt."

"I'm not here for Hitler."

"Oh. Want to try your luck with Marilyn Monroe? We don't sell a tee shirt for this one, but—"

"No!" Willie was sweating now. His heart was pounding, and this guy wouldn't shut up.

"Hey," the man said, raising his hands in surrender, "we're not talking rape here. Our historians just happened to find out about this one party where the sex goddess herself showed up looking for Mr. Right Now, and—"

"*Let me talk!*"

"I'm sorry," the man said with that big smile. "It's just that the possibilities are so endless, we want to make sure you understand your options."

"I know exactly what I want to do."

Willie was sitting forward in the chair now, bouncing a little the way he used to, when he knew a fight was coming. Like his body was going to make sure it was ready, whether he wanted it to or not. And he had the same loose, watery feeling in his bowels, perfect contrast to a mouth so dry he had to clear his throat before he could talk.

It was while Willie was clearing his throat that the man actually lost that smile. Got a sympathetic expression on his face. He reached down somewhere behind him and grabbed a bottle of water. Spoke in gentle tones while Willie drank.

"This is a personal thing, isn't it? Either you want to go back for the one that got away, or you made some huge mistake that you want to fix. Right?"

"Mistake. Big one."

"Don't tell me any details," the man said quickly. "Especially if it involves breaking the law. We have to report anything like that."

"How can you send me—"

"If you've got something specific, something outside our usual packages, all we need are the date and location. What you do there is your business."

Willie nodded. Pulled out his notebook with the date and the GPS coordinates, as near as he could glean the latter from the internet. He started to hand them to the man, but the man put his hands up again.

"Let me give you some advice," the man said. He shook his head. "Don't do this."

"I need to," Willie said, putting every bit of whatever soul he had left into those words.

"All the more reason you shouldn't," the man said. "Look, haven't you—"

"I have to make it right!"

"Haven't you seen the news?"

Willie shook his head.

The man sighed. "Let me put it this way. Today alone, probably two hundred people are going to try to kill Hitler. Hell, a good half of them, at least, will succeed."

Willie was only half-listening. His lips were open now, and he knew he was panting. He was so close now. Why did this man delay him?

"Maybe half as many will try to nail Marilyn Monroe. Or Jane Mansfield. Or somebody like that. Or they'll try to save Jack Kennedy on that day in Texas, and a bunch of them will succeed too. Why do you think so many people can do those things?"

Willie just stared blankly at the man. There was some sense in those words, somewhere, but Willie couldn't puzzle it past his heartbeat.

"You can't change the past," the man said. "Time travel seems to work, but truth is it either creates one hell of a delusion, or it creates alternate timelines. The timeline version is more popular with scientists, but personally I like the delusion angle. It means we aren't messing up whole other worlds just for our own amusement."

Willie was stuck on one sentence there.

"You can't change the past?"

"Nope." The man shook his head firmly. "You could kill Hitler every day for a month, but World War II still happened, complete with death camps. You could seduce Monroe every day for a year, but she'd never leave that night pregnant, no matter how fertile you are. Hell, you could kill Lee Harvey Oswald all you like. He'll still shoot Jack Kennedy."

He leaned forward, his eyes boring right through Willie.

"Whatever you want to go back and change, you can't. You said what you said. You did what you did. My advice? Forget time travel and go see a therapist."

Willie started to get up, but stopped and dropped back down into his chair.

"Wait," Willie said. "You said something about alternate timelines?"

"It's just a theory."

Willie looked at the man until he sighed.

"You can't change *our* past. That's fixed. But some of the scientists, they think that if you go back and make a change, the time stream branches off. Creates a world where whatever you changed becomes *that world's* past."

The man must have seen the light come into Willie's eye, because he rushed to add, "Doesn't change anything here though. You get back to the exact same world you left. Whatever you really did is still what really happened."

"But if I" – Willie saw the man's hands waving him to shut up – "*hypothetically*, went back to a time and place where I could save a bunch of lives—"

"Those people would still be just as dead."

"Here. But in another world…"

The man sighed again. Sagged in his chair. Defeat in his voice as he said, "In another world, maybe – *maybe* – they'll still be alive. If that theory's true. You *may* just be fooling yourself."

Willie gave a helpless shrug.

"That's a chance I have to take."

THE FORGOTTEN REBEL

This story has nothing to do with the American Civil War.

The rebellion in this story is Scots, rebelling against English rule, back at the end of the 13th century. The most famous rebel to come out of this particular period was William Wallace, and not just because of the movie *Braveheart**.

Andrew Moray was another important leader of the Scots at the time, and he played a key role in the Scottish victory at Stirling Bridge. Most reports say he died later that year, though some sources call that into question.

This story takes a look at one way things might've gone down at Stirling Bridge, and what may have happened to Andrew Moray.

*Fun film, though it stole most of Robert the Bruce's thunder and gave it to William Wallace. And it cut Andrew Moray out entirely.

It is widely known that on 11 September 1297, Scottish forces led by William Wallace and Andrew Moray defeated the English invaders led by John de Warenne, the Earl of Surrey, at the Battle of Stirling Bridge.

With Wallace on one side and Moray on the other, the narrow wooden bridge served as a pinch-point, dividing and trapping the English troops and turning what could well have been another victory for Surrey into a resounding defeat.

Surrey knew the bridge was narrow. Furthermore, one of his advisors, Sir Richard Lundie, had offered to ford the river with cavalry two miles upstream, at the same time that the infantry would cross the bridge. An offer that, if accepted, would have given the battle completely different complexion, and possibly a different outcome.

But Surrey's more trusted adviser, Hugh de Cressingham, pushed persuasively for a direct attack across the bridge.

All of that is common knowledge among historians.

What is not common knowledge is the truth of *why* Hugh de Cressingham pressed for a direct attack. And as de Cressingham was killed in the battle, it might well have been the case that no one would ever have learned the truth, if not for one thing: the written testimony of one Charles Morton, who squired for Andrew Moray during the days leading up to the battle.

His account here follows, translated from Early Scots, with language updated for modern readers.

Always so wet near the river Forth. Spray seems to carry for miles, especially this time of year. Makes the cold seep down into your bones, until you don't think you'll ever get warm again.

That kind of chill can make a man sick. Maybe even sick unto death if he isn't careful. And I didn't have just myself to think about this gray evening, but the Moray.

Refused his supper tonight, he did. And he hasn't been out of his tent in many a long hour. I figured him for planning. Going over and over the battle to come. He seemed the type, same as the Wallace. Two men cut from near the same cloth, if I say so myself.

Well, before I went into the Moray's tent tonight, I'd've added no "near" to that sentence. Two of a type they seemed to me. Now, I can only hope I'm wrong on that.

I love Scotland and hate the English, as any true Scot would. I yearn for freedom from the English yoke as much as any patriot.

But still I am a Christian. And what I saw in that tent was anything but Christian.

Bad enough to know what I know about the Moray. I have to hope the same isn't true of the Wallace, or we'll all be damned before we'll ever be free.

I was approaching the Moray's tent to see if I could tempt him with a little stew, when I heard noises from within. Sounded like he was talking to someone, in low tones. Secret talk, maybe, but there was nothing wrong with that. Commander's got a right to issue his orders how he pleases.

Just to be sure, I called to old Joc Dundee, who was sharpening his sword by the nearby fire again. Never understood why his sword needed so much sharpening. Joc was half a bear himself. Could've killed just as fast with those big paws of his.

"Hey, Joc," I said. "Who's that in there with himself?"

Joc just shook his head. "The Moray keeps his own counsel tonight."

Some might have been troubled by that. A man talking to himself. But me, my gran always said, "when a man gets too many worries, he talks to himself more than he will anyone else." And with the English coming, the Moray had a right to his worries. So I didn't think anything of it.

"Dinner, sir," I called at the flap of his tent, then went straight in the way I always have, letting the flap fall closed behind me.

The Moray was on his knees, bare to the chest and surrounded by burning candles. Sweating, he was. And now I think on it, does seem to me that the tent was more than passing warm, which didn't make any sense at all. But it wasn't much of a care at the time.

More concerning, the Moray had some kind of a device drawn on his chest in what I devoutly hope was red wax from the candles. If it was blood…

Anyway, that symbol, it were drawn again on parchment hanging from the side of the tent before him, like he was trying to stare it down while he mumbled to himself.

Well, there's no point in playing around about it. He wasn't mumbling. He was chanting. Just doing it soft like, so no one would hear what he was saying.

Not that hearing the words clearly would have helped. Even standing there just inside the tent, my mouth hanging open wide enough to let a whole troop of cavalry come marching down my tongue, I could hear the sounds he was making right plain.

But they weren't any words I could recognize.

Now, I speak Scots as well as any man. Some English too. And I know the sound of good Church Latin when I hear it. What the Moray was speaking, though, it wasn't any of those.

Only thing I could think didn't make any sense to me. The Moray, he's no highlander to be speaking Gaelic. Was all I could think, though, and I didn't have much time to put any worry into it beyond that.

Soon as he realized I was there, the Moray turned his gaze on me.

Much as I love and respect the man, that gaze, it didn't seem human. It were like being stared into by Satan himself. His eyes seemed to burn brighter than the candles, and I swear to Saint Peter I could *feel* his stare on me like a slap to the face.

Had to shake my head to clear it, and by the time I did, the Moray was on his feet, buttoning up his shirt and standing in front of … whatever that parchment on the side of the tent was. That fire was gone from his eyes like it had never been there.

"What do you want?" he asked me, voice so rough you'd've thought he'd been yelling orders all day.

I held up the bowl of stew. "Need your strength … for tomorrow … sir."

He smiled then, and it was his usual smile. Confident. Inspiring. The smile that made men follow him.

"Bring it here," he rasped, though his voice sounded stronger as he continued, "I find I've a powerful hunger."

I don't mind admitting my hands were shaking as I carried the bowl to himself. And I couldn't help noticing the way he shifted on his feet to keep that parchment on the tent wall from my eyes, which couldn't help looking for it.

My head, it was swimming. The heat. The gaze. The chanting. The candles, which were still lit and still surrounding the Moray, even if he ignored them like they weren't there.

Thinking on it now, I realize that part of me was trying to deny what I saw. Trying to tell me that I hadn't seen, heard, nor felt anything out of the ordinary.

But I've been keeping this journal for years now, and I've been setting everything down as true as true could be. And I think maybe that habit made me face the truth of what I'd seen.

The Moray's a witch.

And himself, for all his smiling, I think he saw that in my eyes as I approached.

Soon as I got close enough to offer him the soup, the Moray took the bowl with one hand and clapped his grip on the back of my neck with the other. Powerful grip he had. Felt as though I couldn't move any part of myself.

"What did you see?" he asked, tone so casually attentive he might have been asking the scouts to report.

But his words, they were echoing in my head, right along with those parts of me trying to tell me I hadn't seen anything unusual. That I'd just caught him at his prayers, and that was all.

I licked my lips. I think I even wanted to tell him that bit about the prayers, because I wanted to tell him what he wanted to hear. I know part of me wanted to believe it.

But as I looked into those commanding eyes of his, the truth came pouring past my lips. The device, the chanting in a strange tongue, the candles, all of it.

The Moray frowned. Kept that one hand on the back of my neck, but set down the bowl. And as Saint Michael is my witness, I swear that the Moray put his hand on the hilt of his knife. He could have killed me then, and I could have made no move to stop him. But he paused short of drawing that blade.

The Moray frowned. "Do I hear old Joc sharpening his sword?"

I had to try to hear past the pounding of my heart, but soon as I heard that scaping sound, I nodded.

"Saw you come in, didn't he?"

"I asked him if you had company."

The Moray shook his head and let go of my neck. And I swear by all the saints that I felt released. Like as though my whole body had been stretched on the rack. And when the Moray let go of my neck, I nearly collapsed on the dirt.

The Moray shook his head again and spoke to me in a low voice.

"I need you to understand something, Morton. What I do, I do for Scotland."

"It's witchcraft, sir. It's—"

"Going to guarantee us victory tomorrow, is what it'll do. I've sent a dream this night to Hugh de Cressingham. A powerful dream. It will convince him that the path to victory is the one that just happens to play straight into our hands."

"But—"

"Why not go straight for Surrey?" The Moray shook his head. "Surrey's beyond my reach. But de Cressingham isn't, and he's a talker. He'll persuade Surrey."

I wasn't going to ask him a question though. I only had a simple statement in mind, and I spoke it then.

"But, sir. It's witchcraft."

"If you let that truth out, Morton, morale will break. Our unity will splinter. Scotland will fall before we've even risen, and England will hold us in its grip forever. Is that what you want?"

"Of course not, sir," I said, but then it was my turn to shake my head. "But if we win our freedom without God on our side, we've won nothing but our own damnation."

The Moray sighed.

"Give me this much then," he said. "Say nothing of what you've seen this night. Let us beat Surrey tomorrow, and after the battle I'll disappear. I swear it. I'll give all leadership to William Wallace, a man every bit as Christian as you. Let him lead Scotland to freedom."

I bit my lip. My silence would make me complicit, and might endanger my soul.

"Don't do this for me, boy," the Moray said. "Do it for Scotland."

That decided me. What was done was done, and my talking about it wouldn't change it.

"For Scotland, sir," I said, and saluted.

He dismissed me then. I finished my duties and came back here to write. I can only pray I've made the right decision.

OFFICIAL ACCOUNTS DIFFER AS TO THE FATE OF ANDREW MORAY. SOME say he was slain at the Battle of Stirling Bridge. Others say he was wounded, and died of his wounds during November that year.

The truth is not known to official historians, nor, alas, is it known to this writer. One thing is certain: Andrew Moray disappeared from the war for Scottish independence following the Battle of Stirling Bridge.

He began the war as a major leader and left it as a footnote, compared to the legends of William Wallace and Robert the Bruce.

Charles Morton died on 22 July 1298 at the battle of Falkirk. His journals, along with his remains, were delivered to his family at Lothian. The journals were turned over to historians at the time, excepting the journal containing Morton's account of the night before the Battle of Stirling Bridge.

The Morton family claimed that the volume had been lost in transit.

However, the Morton family in Scotland was never powerful enough to become a clan in their own right. They were known to be a sept of the much more powerful Douglas clan. And it was the practice at the time that the remains of all Scottish soldiers were organized by clan first and family second.

Thus, the journals of Charles Morton found their way into the hands of the Douglas clan, where Sir Archibald Douglas held back that volume, as a potential political weapon, in case the Moray family became rivals.

The journal was not used this way, and might have disappeared entirely, were it not discovered at auction in the late nineteenth century by Samuel Liddell MacGregor Mathers, occultist and known member of the Golden Dawn.

Mathers, alas, failed to draw serious academic interest in the journal. But its truth survives to this day.

STARING DOWN THE BARREL OF A WAND

I love the Beastie Boys. All their albums, hell, pretty much every track.

On the day I wrote this story, I had the song "Looking Down the Barrel of a Gun" going through my head.

I considered writing an homage, to be honest. The story of a car thief on a night gone horribly wrong. Instead, I wondered what would happen if I changed the gun to a wand. After all, it seemed to me that opening a detective story with a guy looking down the barrel of a gun was probably a trope.

So why not twist is a bit? This story was the result.

The grin was fake. The wand was all too real.

Jake looked like he shouldn't know which end of a wand to hold. Built like a tombstone, and just about as bright. Couldn't even find a decent tailor for that suit. Who wears pinstripes anymore?

The wand, though. Looked like teak, and there's a reason people say "teak means trouble." Already had a red spark at the end, like Jake was itching for a reason. Or thought he already had one.

I was betting on the latter.

No backup with him though. Maybe meant it was off the books. Which was something. Not much, but something. I could work with it.

Just him and me, in the back of Tony's. Under the unforgiving light of the fluorescent ceiling lamps.

A goddamn restaurant storeroom. Should have had places to hide. Maybe a teetering crate I could tip. But not Tony's. Never Tony's. Storeroom as spick and span as the restaurant itself.

I mean even the roaches must have wiped their feet before setting foot back here.

No, there was only one place to hide in Tony's storeroom, and the last thing I wanted to do was call Jake's attention to it.

What else did I have to work with? Not much. Couple of toys in my pockets, but nothing that'd stand up to teak. Racks of cleaning supplies behind me. Simple, chemical stuff. No thaum, but maybe something useful if the first blast doesn't get me.

Crates to my right, stacked against the wall. Like maybe I could climb them, if I were fast enough. And if I could fit through that little window up above.

I'm fast. And I'm a skinny guy. But not that skinny. And I'm not sure anybody's *that* fast.

Two exits then. Doors. One to the outside. Back alley I knew pretty well. Closed. Maybe locked. Wouldn't have time to do anything about that, if it were.

The other, the door into the restaurant. Closed, but likely unlocked.

Both those doors, on the other side of Tony.

"I smell marinara," I said, and it was true. "Do you smell marinara? Tony makes the best meatballs in the city, Jake. What say I buy you a sub and you tell me what's—"

"Didja think I wouldn't find out, Carlo? I ain't that dumb."

The second part of that I wouldn't touch for a million. Not with Jake holding teak on me like he might be able to make it do more than spark. The first part though…

"Now, Jake," I said stretching my fake grin a little wider, and pretending my heart wasn't already trying to flee down that back alley, "it's not that I was keeping secrets from you. It's just that this was supposed to be part of your big birthday surprise, and—"

"What are you talking about?"

"Nothing." I blinked fast. Dropped the grin like it was never there. Tried to pretend I wasn't sweating. "What are *you* talking about?"

"You keep away from…" Jake frowned. The tip of the wand stopped dropping sparks for a moment. "What's this about my birthday?"

Wait. Was his birthday really approaching? And here I had a line all ready to go about advanced planning, so "he wouldn't be suspicious."

Think fast, Carlo.

"Look," I said, raising my hands a little higher, like I'd never lie to a guy holding a wand on me. "I don't know nothing about your birthday. Couldn't even tell you when it is. I just know that Petey Boy gave me a sharp deadline for … what I'm supposed to do…" – I winked at Jake, as though I'd actually work for scum like Peter "Petey Boy" Mariucci – "and he made it clear that if I ruined your birthday surprise, they'd be cleaning up bits of my soul for the next century."

The threat was one I'd really heard Petey Boy make once. And from what I knew of the *stregas* working for Petey Boy, I'd believe it.

And from the look on Jake's face, he believed it too. He lowered the wand. Frowned. Bobbed his head left and right, thinking, but that shellacked black hair of his never moved.

He slipped the wand up his sleeve.

What was that taste? Air? Just how long had I been holding my breath?

Jake shot his cuffs, as though that would make them straight on that ill-fitting piece of crap he called a suit.

Shrugged his shoulders. Straightened his matching tie. Held up a threatening finger.

"Well, you got a job for Petey Boy, and you better do it right or I'll mess you up before he finishes off what's left."

"No problem, Jake," I said, grin back in place.

Jake actually started to turn away, but shook himself and turned back. Gave me an even darker look. Twitched his arm like he was going for the wand, but changed his mind. Held up a closed fist instead.

"And you stay the hell away from Alison. You hear me?"

"Alison who, Jake?" I sounded like the soul of innocence, if I do say so myself.

"You know damn well, Alison who. Alison McGillicuddy."

"Jake," I said, in as close to an admonishing tone as I dared right then, "you know me and Alison are ancient history. I haven't seen her since—"

"Keep it that way," Jake said, his frown deepening. "Or Petey Boy'll have to get someone else to arrange my birthday surprise. And it better be a good one."

Jake adjusted his shoulders again, but it didn't help the fit of his suit. He strode out, heels of his loafers clicking on the polished wood of Tony's storeroom floor.

I think I caught my first full breath when Jake closed the restaurant door behind him.

Damn near had a heart attack when I heard the next click, but it was just Alison coming out of Tony's secret bathroom.

Tony was a germaphobe. Paranoid enough that he had a personal bathroom back here that even his employees didn't know about. Disguised to look like part of the wall, without a drop of thaum. Pretty clever. Most people'd never think to look for a mundane hiding place. Not at Tony's, anyway.

I only knew about it because it played a key role in my helping Tony find out who was stealing from his safe last year.

Safe was in Tony's office now. But the bathroom remained.

And out of that bathroom came an angel. My angel. Or at least, she used to be.

Alison McGillicuddy.

Looked as Irish as her name. Copper curls and freckles, but skin like a soap commercial and a body worth facing down teak for. Even in jeans and a turtleneck, she looked hot enough to melt Tony's kitchen freezer from where she was standing.

But I had no right to think about her that way. Not anymore.

Not to mention that saying anything so crass around Tony might have gotten me a heap full of trouble. Tony treated Alison like the daughter he never had. Only reason *she* knew about Tony's special bathroom.

"You see, Carlo?" Alison said in the smoky voice that made her singing so popular. "Not even one date, and already he thinks he owns me. I can't take it anymore. I can't take singing in these mob bars. Putting up with mob come-ons, and the consequences of saying no. I need to get out of this town."

"You're holding out on me," I said, trying to resist the pull of those green eyes. She wasn't an *actual* angel – far as I knew – but the woman had some fae in her bloodline, or my name wasn't Carlo Genovese. "How the hell is Jake handling teak these days?"

"The Mouse is dead. Petey Boy moved Jake up to fill the opening. Got him a higher initiation and everything."

Two big points wrapped in one simple sentence. Jake getting moved up should have been the one grabbing my attention, but the other was too unexpected.

The Mouse was dead?

Nastiest outfit hitter in the city. Got his nickname back when he was starting out, for being small and quiet. Kept it because it amused him, even while he piled up a body count like a Civil War battlefield.

"When did this happen?"

"It doesn't matter," Alison said. "Jake's Petey Boy's right hand killer now. And he wants *me*. Please help me, Carlo."

"What aren't you telling me?"

"Nothing that could hurt you. Believe me, you're better off not knowing. And once I'm gone, it won't matter." She fluttered her eyelashes at me. "You're the only one who can help me, Carlo. The only one I can trust. I'll pay you whatever you want."

She knew I wouldn't take her money. Just like she knew I wouldn't say no. Even though it meant crossing Jake. Which, given Jake's new role, meant crossing Petey Boy, if I wasn't very, very careful.

But I could never say no to Alison.

Lots of folks don't like cemeteries at night.

Me, I don't mind 'em at night. At night my spirit eyes are better. I can see where to step and where not to. I can spot trouble before it spots me. Much of the time, anyway.

No, for me, cemeteries are worse during the day. The lamentations of the living, coping with loss. The dead, harder to see, and generally crankier under the harsh summer sun.

But not even for Alison was I going to go into this thing blind.

Thus, from Tony's I went to Saint Helena's. Locally called the Cemetery of the Unwanted. Looked the part. As much dirt as crabgrass, and half of the trees should have had graves of their own. Whole place was as flat, depressing and pointless as nonalcoholic beer.

The fat, rosy-cheeked priest was giving a Latin mass for a junkie. Seemed excessive to me, but Father Roland never buried anyone without their propers.

Only three attendees – not including me, way at the back, leaning against a dead oak. Junkies. Friends of the deceased, I supposed. They looked ready for coffins of their own. Soon as they stopped twitching and scratching.

The priest, the junkies, that was all side-stuff. My line of work, it paid to notice everything around me. Center of my attention was the gravedigger. Watkins. Wasn't his real name. We all knew it. But he was part of the "names are power" crowd, so we called him Watkins anyway.

Colombian fella. Pushing sixty hard enough that he may have been doing it for a couple of decades, but he still had a full head of gray hair that matched that thick mustache, and the kind of dumpy frame that all the doctors say is bad for you, even though Watkins never took a sick day that anyone I knew ever heard of.

Watkins finally felt my stare. Looked up. I nodded. He nodded back.

Bowed his head over his shovel again. Muttered the right responses at the right times in the service.

I stepped away and lit up an herbal. Blend of wild ginger, mandrake, and a couple of other things that help me stay just a little luckier than the people chasing me. That was the theory, anyway. Way my luck was running though, maybe I needed fresher ginger.

I had plenty of time to smoke before the service ended, when I could talk to Watkins while he shoveled dirt, old school style. Said it helped ease the passage for the dead.

But Watkins was a necromancer. And if he wanted to shovel grave dirt the old fashioned way, no one was going to question it. Least of all, me.

I was still approaching the open grave when Watkins started talking to me. He was already shoveling dirt. Slowly, like each shovelful had meaning.

"Black suit," he said. "You're learning, Carlo."

"Didn't want to seem disrespectful," I said, while my eyes scanned the graveyard. No other funerals going right then, but I was pretty sure I spotted someone who didn't want to be seen. Skinny boy, over by a living elm tree at the other end of the cemetery.

I noted him. Hopefully without tipping that I did.

But Watkins was still talking about my suit.

"More like you wanted to get on my good side. I saw you make an offering at the entrance."

"What, I can't just be polite?" My smile was real enough, but that was just because I liked Watkins. And the offering was just a little something so the dead might look on me a little more favorably. I tended to need all the help I could get.

Watkins paused to give me a simple look. No force or accusation in those caramel eyes of his. More like patience. Like he was waiting for me to cut the crap.

"I need information," I said. "And I can pay."

"Money?" Watkins said the word like it was obscene.

"Hey, most of us need it to live," I said. "But if you want something else, we can work it out, depending on the value of the information." I shrugged. "Of course, there's still the matter of that beagle that went missing two weeks ago. I don't think I ever sent a bill for that..."

The beagle was Cleaver. Watkins' ... well, I wasn't sure if familiar was the right word or not, but it was as close as I could come to understanding. It had been dognapped by some idiots on the east side. I probably did *them* as much of a favor as I did Watkins by getting the dog back with no muss or fuss.

Stealing from a necromancer. Not exactly a bright move. But if everybody played smart all the time, I'd never have any work.

"Already pointing out that I owe you," Watkins said with a sigh. His voice was so casual, I could almost miss that he was doing a little something with each shovelful of dirt. And if it wasn't my imagination, it was a kind of blessing. "Just what do you need to know?"

"Not sure," I admitted. "And that's the worst part. I've got three things coming together all at once. The Mouse is dead..."

Watkins didn't even twitch at that news. Was I the last to know? Or was it just because nobody died in this town without him knowing?

"Jake's got his job, and Jake's running around with teak now. Finally, Alison wants out of town."

"The Mouse was a murder," Watkins said. "Poison. *If* Petey Boy doesn't know that now, he will soon."

Watkins was silent for another shovelful of dirt, then glanced at me as he scattered it down into the hole, onto the coffin.

"Jake's initiation's the real thing."

That part just didn't come together for me. Power and IQ didn't always go hand-in-hand, but I'd crossed Jake before, a few years back. I had a sense of his scope. White hawthorn should have been beyond him. Much less teak.

I shook my head. "How the hell did—"

"How do you think?" Watkins stopped shoveling for a moment and looked at me. "Obviously I wasn't involved. So how can *I* be *one hundred percent* certain of his initiation?"

Watkins went back to shoveling while the implication of his words hit me like dirt slapping down onto that junkie's coffin.

Human sacrifice? That would have been enough to get even Jake an initiation to the teak. And death magic like that, no way it could happen in this town without Watkins feeling it.

But why would Petey Boy waste a life for Jake? I mean, apart from the fact that human sacrifice was a *federal* crime, to be powerful the person had to be important to Petey Boy. If he was going to sacrifice someone, he could have benefitted himself more...

"The Mouse," I whispered. "The Mouse was going to move against Petey Boy, but Petey Boy moved first."

"Not saying that's right," Watkins said. "But it does sound like the way to bet."

"Where does Alison fit into all this?"

Cleaver came up then, barking like he had something important on his mind. Watkins turned and listened to his ... dog. I'm just going to say dog. Cleaver may or may not have been a familiar, but he was definitely a dog.

Watkins and Cleaver turned to look at me in perfect sync.

Watkins frowned.

"What?" I asked, but Watkins shook his head. Once, sharp and sudden.

Watkins and Cleaver just melted into the dirt like they were made of week-old snow. The shovel fell to the now-empty ground.

"How the..." I started, but instinct took over. I dove for the crabgrass.

Just in time. A blast of power singed the air right where I'd been standing. Too distracted with my Q&A. Stupid. Stupid.

Didn't even get to see which way the blast came from. Needed a moment to get my bearings.

I rolled right into the open grave.

Six feet might not sound like a long distance, but falling six feet down onto a coffin knocked the wind out of me. Even ready for it, as I was.

Found my feet before I found my air. Sprinkled a little *hop-hop* powder on my shoes. Crouched and waited.

The moment a face leaned over the grave, I leaped. The *hop-hop* powder turned my normal ten inch vertical into more like ten feet.

I plowed fist first through the jaw of my assailant on my way past.

Up and up, then coming straight down onto the patchy crabgrass and rough, dry dirt.

Terrible for my suit, but not the worst surface to hit at a roll.

Had my air back as I came to my feet. Got a good look at my assailant. The skinny kid from over by the elm. Up close now he looked like he should have been working in a big box store. Khakis and a red polo shirt. Even had the short brown hair for it. All he needed was a nametag.

Still. He must have slipped close when I wasn't watching. Sloppy, sloppy, Carlo.

He was sitting on the dirt right then, shaking his head like he was trying to drive off a whole Milky Way of stars. The little stick of ash forgotten on the ground beside him.

I snatched it up, then kicked him across the jaw, for good measure. Laid him out flat, but still conscious.

"You can take a hit pretty good, kid," I said, twirling his wand in my fingers. "Too bad your aim sucks."

My witty repartee, such as it was, was wasted. The kid was still too dazzled from back-to-back shots to the chin.

I dragged him over to the dead oak, where I'd waited during the service. Leaned him against it.

"Put your hands up," I said.

He did it like he thought I was threatening him, which was probably not the worst thing for me. But it did help him get his senses back on the world around him, instead of off in the solar system somewhere.

"Care to tell me why you were trying to put me underground?"

The kid sneered the way only the young can. Had to have been a decade younger than me. Maybe not even old enough to drink. What a waste.

"Start talking, or you know what this wand can do..." I gave him a smile.

"You're dead either way, Genovese." Christ, this kid's voice hadn't finished changing yet. Either that, or somebody clipped him somewhere unpleasant. Voice as high as his just wasn't natural.

"Threats won't help."

"Not a threat," he said, giving me the slow head shake, like he thought he had gravitas. "Jake put out the word. If you were doing anything other than getting his birthday surprise ready for tonight, he—"

"*Tonight?*"

What was I saying about the direction of my luck lately?

"Yeah," the kid said with a shrug. "The birthday party." Then the kid smiled. "Oh, fuck. You *lied* to Jake? Don't you know who he is now, man?"

Wands don't have to kill. No matter what most people say about them. Yeah, they're pretty much limited to slinging around energy one way or another, and yeah, only the really big muckety-mucks can use them to make objects sit up and dance and all that jazz.

But just because a wand can *blast*, didn't mean it had to *kill*.

And me, I had just a little more finesse than the Jakes of this world.

So I laid the kid out with a quick zap, that would keep him stacking z's until the wee morning hours. Well after it was too late for him to carry any word to Jake. I slipped his wand up my sleeve. I didn't like carrying wands. Too tempting. But the way this day was going...

Jake's birthday party was tonight?

No way Alison wasn't due to sing at it. And they'd expect her early, to get dressed and set up. Mic checks. Whole nine. They'd send a car for her...

That meant I had no more than four hours to get Alison out of town. Any longer might be too late.

Four hours.

IF I COULD HAVE JUST PUT ALISON ON A BUS, I WOULD HAVE. HELL, OR A plane, train, boat, even a taxi. I didn't care. I'd've paid Watson a big chunk just to have him ship her out through the Underworld, if it meant I could get her out of town right now.

But no. Alison was a singer, and she was under contract to a band. Or, to be more specific, to the band's manager. Sparky Johannsson.

If Alison would have been willing to quit singing, she could have skipped scot-free anytime she wanted. But Alison giving up singing, that would be like me giving up looking for trouble.

Even if I wanted to, I couldn't do it.

So my first stop after the cemetery was a three story brownstone in the part of town we called the Village. I think maybe it was the first site of settlers in the area, or something. If that's not it, then I had no idea where it got the nickname.

Either way, the bottom floor of the brownstone was the kind of Chinese laundry that worked with Taoist sorcery to clean a lot more than the cemetery stains on my suit. They'd clean all foreign influences. Bring my clothes, and through my clothes me, more fully into harmony with the universe.

But I didn't have that kind of money to spend on dry cleaning.

Second floor was all one big law office. Now, I'm not as big on the "names are power" bit as guys like Watkins, but I try not to utter aloud the names of any lawyers, just in case it means they can hear me. So forgive me for not naming the office. Suffice to say it was big, and I definitely didn't want their attention.

The third floor had a dance studio, an insurance group, and Johannsson Talent Services.

Johannsson was the kind of guy who had his office door warded against creditors. Pretty much said everything I needed to know about him.

I didn't knock.

The blonde behind the desk was a guy. Another kid around drinking age. Looked like he was going for the world record in beard length.

"Geez," he said, before I could even get the full lay of the land, "you smell like you've been playing rugby." Looked askance at my suit. "Look like it too."

"Something like that," I said. The office smelled like mothballs and gin. Filing cabinets against one wall. Metal ones, that locked. Big posters on the cream stucco walls, of gigs his artists had done. A big orange couch sitting between potted plants that had seen better days. Which was sad. I mean, how hard is it to keep a ficus going?

The blonde guy stared at me. Like all the niceties of office work were supposed to be implied, and I was supposed to get right on with telling him what I wanted.

No manners. Kids these days.

"I want to see Sparky," I said.

"So does most of the city," Blondie Boy said, looking at my suit again and shaking his head. "Do you have an appointment?"

And that's when I cheated.

I flipped my favorite coin. Made it myself. Silver on one side, gold on the other. Moon metal and sun metal, part of the same coin. With all the right sigils carved into each side, under the pure light that fit the side.

The coin spun fast in the air. Caught Blondie Boy's attention, and dazzled him with the rapid fire switch from sun to moon and back.

I caught the coin. Blondie Boy looked at me, his face wrinkled up in confusion.

"What was I saying?" he asked.

"You were *apologizing* for not writing down my appointment, when I made it yesterday."

"Your ... appointment?"

"Yes," I said firmly. "*My appointment with Sparky.* It's set for *right now.*"

"Appointment ... right now..." Blondie Boy shook himself. "I'm so sorry, sir. I don't know how I could have made a mistake like that. Just knock and go right in."

I deliberately forgot all about the knock part and walked straight into the only inner office in the place. Sparky's.

It was a big office. Huge bearskin rug in the middle. Half a dozen big, comfy office chairs on one side of a giant of an oak desk, and an executive chair on the other side that made the other chairs look pathetic.

Speaking of pathetic...

Sparky was naked on the bearskin rug right now, and giving it to a redhead who couldn't have been any older than Blondie Boy, and indeed might have been his sister. Both were sweaty and smelly with what they'd been doing.

But the moment I stepped in, Sparky looked up and yelled, "What the hell?"

"Nice soundproofing," I said, meandering in toward the nicer set of filing cabinets in here. These were oak, to match the desk, and I was betting anything worth finding was going to be inside them. I could practically smell their wards.

Under the smells of ... well, you know...

"Who are you?" Sparky said, jumping to his feet. Naked as the huge guy was, he looked like he was already wearing a bear skin of his own. Still, he threw on a purple silk robe, for which I was grateful.

The redhead didn't bother getting up. Just looked at me like I was a curiosity worthy of study. Normally, a woman that hot and naked giving me the eye would have distracted me. But given what she'd just been doing, and with whom, I had no trouble keeping my attention on Sparky.

"I'm..."

"Carlo Genovese," the redhead said, surprising me.

"Genovese," Sparky said, like he was trying to remember the name. "Actor?"

"Troublemaker," the redhead said.

"I'm sorry," I said, meeting the redhead's eyes and keeping my gaze right there while speaking to her. "You seem to have me at a disadvantage."

"I'm the one who's naked," she said.

"What are you doing here?" Sparky said. "And make it fast."

"Look," I said, turning my attention back to Sparky with a smile that was supposed to put everyone at ease, but probably didn't. "If you can be reasonable, then I'll be out of your hair in no time, and you can go back to playing with your ingenue."

Both of them started laughing at me.

I hate it when people laugh at me.

"I like that," the redhead said. "*Ingenue.* If I'm an ingenue, you should be paying me more, Sparky."

"I'm paying you enough," Sparky said, not looking at the redhead. To me, he spoke in a careful voice, like maybe he knew who I was after all. "All right, Genovese. You pulled something on poor Marco out there, so whatever you have to say must be important. Spill it quick."

"I want you to tear up Alison McGillicuddy's contract. That fast enough for you?"

The redhead whistled.

"Quiet, you," Sparky said. Then frowned. "Alison's a big act for me. I might let you buy out her contract, if you can make it worth my while. Won't be cheap though."

"You think *Genovese* has that kind of money?" the redhead said.

Just who was this woman? I mean, besides the obvious.

"Money's not a good option," I said. "What else would you want for that contract?"

"Money's always the best option," Sparky said, and went to sit behind his desk. Steepled his fingers, with his elbows on all that oak.

"You sure you don't just want to get cash? I don't care how you get it, as long as it doesn't trace back to me."

Class act all the way, this Johannsson.

"Come on, Sparky," I said. "If you're not going to be reasonable, I might have to get heavy."

"He means it," the redhead said. "Genovese may be broke more often than not, but if he comes at a guy, he tends not to miss."

"All right," I said to the redhead. "Seriously. Who are you?"

She just smiled at me. Something about that smile bothered me.

"Talk to *me*, Genovese," Sparky said. Then frowned. Moved his head like he was running numbers in his mind. "All right, look. I've ... had a run of bad luck at cards."

The redhead started laughing, which shook her in a way that could be all too distracting. I focused as hard on Sparky as I could.

"Shut up, you," Sparky said. To me, he said, "I'm into the guys at the Blue Dollar Club for a fair chunk. If you can get them to forgive the debt, I'll give you Alison's contract. Then you can do what you want with it."

Get a mob casino man to forgive a debt? Getting Watkins to perform human sacrifice would have been easier. But then, I was already trying to get *one* person out of town anyway...

"Look," I said. "What if you split town? Not like these guys can affect your credit rating."

"And give up my contacts? Forget it."

"Plus me," the redhead said, pulling up the bearskin rug around her in a way that covered her, but looked like it didn't. "You know you couldn't go a week without me, Sparky."

The redhead smiled at Sparky, and I could see his eyes glaze just a bit. Fix on her. She stared back like she was staring through him. Like snakes stare at their prey.

I felt it then. Just a touch. A whisper.

Power.

This redhead. She wasn't even a little bit human.

I uncapped a tube of salt I keep in my jacket, and spun a quick circle around the redhead on the bearskin rug before she could get to her feet to stop me.

She hissed. Sparky just stared. A touch of drool started dripping out of the corner of his mouth.

"I was doing you a *favor*, Genovese," the redhead said, but I wasn't listening. I didn't need favors from the likes of her. I chanted a binding in the fastest Latin I could spit, while still getting the words right.

But the time I was done, the redhead still looked like she could have been gracing the pages of a men's magazine. If that men's magazine liked women with fangs, horns and bat wings, plus talons instead of fingernails.

The binding snapped into place, with a feeling like a sharp sudden stillness to the air. Sparky shook his head, every bit as confused at the moment as Blondie Boy had been by my favorite coin.

The succubus hissed again.

Sparky got a good look at what he'd actually been bumping uglies with. Paled up right to the bald spot.

No doubt he was also finally feeling the loss of the life force she'd been sucking out of him. What with her bound in a salt circle, unable to hide it from him.

"So," I said to Sparky. "You get her from Dave Greenie?"

"Yeah," Sparky said slowly.

I shook my head. "Don't you know anything? Greenie's been busted twice for using succubi. Last time, the tip came from me." I turned to the succubus. "That's why you knew so much about me."

"I was doing you a favor, Genovese." Seemed unfair that something as evil as that succubus could sound so sexy. "Sparky'd never let go of Alison. Thinks he's in love with her."

So he hired redheaded prostitutes? So he could pretend they were her? Made sense. Alison'd never touch a sleaze like Sparky here.

"Love burns you, doesn't it?" I asked with a smile. "The more he's been falling, the less fun you're having sucking down his soul."

The succubus hissed.

I shook my head again. Turned to Sparky. "Look. Don't ever go to Dave Greenie, all right? You want to hire a girl, go to Tina Polanski."

"Know all about prostitutes, do you Genovese?" the succubus said. "No love since you lost your angel?"

I didn't hurt women. And the succubus looked enough like a woman that my reflexes made the thought unpleasant. But I was tempted.

Sparky looked up at me. Crestfallen.

"How long's she been feeding off you?" I asked.

"Two months now. Twice a week. Three times, when ... when..." – he mumbled the last part, but I could make it out – "when Alison has a gig."

"Alison's a dead end for you," I said softly. "You know that, right?"

He nodded. Tears now. Just what I needed.

The succubus laughed at Sparky. I pulled a tissue from the box on his desk. Looked away while he cleaned up.

"You and me, Sparky," I said softly, leaning in as close as I could comfortably lean. "We need to forget about Alison. There's out of our league, then there's *way* out of our league. You know?"

"But..." Sparky started, but I cut him off.

"If you tear up her contract," I said, "I'll get her out of town. Today. You'll never have to see her again. Maybe you can move on. Maybe we both can."

Sparky needed more convincing than that. Took longer than I was happy with. Guy just wasn't ready to live without at least a little of Alison in his life.

But in the end, he agreed. I think it was the succubus laughing at him that made the difference.

When he tore up Alison's contract, I smiled at the succubus.

"Want me to banish her for you? Send her back to hell?"

"No," Sparky said slowly. "I've got a friend who specializes in just this kind of thing."

From the tone of Sparky's voice, I got the feeling that the trip home was going to be more than a little uncomfortable for the succubus. Somehow, I couldn't bring myself to feel sorry for her.

Besides, I now had just over two hours to get Alison out of town.

FAR AS I KNEW, NO ONE WAS TAILING ME WHEN I LEFT THAT brownstone. But after that little incident in the cemetery, I wasn't willing to take the chance that I'd missed something. So I spent part of the precious time I had left throwing a few false trails and planting fake leads. Some with a touch of thaum for verisimilitude. Others, just good old fashioned legwork. If I did all that right – and this was the kind of thing I was really good at – once I picked up Alison, I could walk her down Main Street and no one would be able to follow us.

Then it wasn't much more than a matter of picking up a ticket for a train leaving about thirty minutes before I figured the window would close on getting Alison out of town. Before anyone would notice that she wasn't where she was supposed to be.

Sure, the ticket was only coach, but like the succubus said, funds weren't my strong suit.

Then one more stop, just to make sure of a few things, and all I had to do was pick up Alison, get her on that train, and as of around midnight she'd be down in Springfield and out of my life forever.

No way it was going to be that easy.

Alison was smart enough not to meet me at her apartment. I mean, me showing up at Alison's? The day Jake-the-newly-promoted tells me to stay away from her?

I'm good, but even I have limits.

We used the back of Tony's again.

I still hated those fluorescent lamps overhead, but the smell of Tony's marinara made up for a lot. Maybe it would even keep me from smelling Alison's perfume, if I got close enough.

Probably not. Better to not get close enough to find out.

She was waiting when I entered the storeroom. Dressed just the way she was earlier, except now the turtleneck and jeans had been joined by a pea coat. And even in that she looked sexy.

I ... I still looked like I'd been dragged here by a horse. Hadn't had time to change, or even clean up. Not and do everything I had to do. But I did have a red carnation in the buttonhole, now. Might have made me look a little fancier, anyway.

"Well?" she asked, the moment she saw me. All eagerness in those green eyes.

"Tore the contract up in front of me," I said with a smile, and the smile I got in return made me want to keep up the warm feelings, so I kept talking. Like an idiot.

"Got the train ticket right here," I said, holding it up. "All we got to do..." I hesitated, looking around for what I didn't see. What I really, really hoped I'd see. "All we..."

My stomach sank. I felt a wave of cold run down my neck.

"Alison, where are your bags?"

I heard the click, and this time I knew immediately what it was. And who.

I turned to Tony's "secret" restroom, and saw Petey Boy Mariucci strut out with a smile as oily as his salt-and-pepper hair. Petey Boy was probably twice my age, but still whip thin, and looked like he'd enjoy doing his own dirty work.

Unlike Jake, though, Petey Boy had taste. Had to give him that much. Dark blue suit that probably cost more than a decade's rent for the likes of me. Hell, that soft blue tie probably cost more than I spent on clothes all year.

And his shoes. I could smell the quality of the leather.

And, it seemed, there was his taste in women.

Petey Boy walked over and put his arm around Alison, who snuggled right in like it was the perfect fit.

I didn't expect Jake to come walking out of that bathroom, following Petey Boy, but I probably should have.

All of them were smiling at me. Laughing, with their eyes.

I itched to go for the ash wand up my sleeve. I could blast Mariucci. Maybe even Jake before Jake could pull and aim that teak of his.

Wrong play, but tempting, with the wand so ready at hand. Had to flex my fingers to keep from doing it.

"Guess my birthday surprise worked out okay after all," Jake said, and then the others were laughing with more than their eyes. "You should see your face, Genovese."

"The carnation is a lovely touch," Petey Boy said in those precise tones of his. "But I fear it does little to mitigate your odor. What *have* you been doing today?"

"Wasting my time," I said, crumpling the carnation in my hand and dropping it to Tony's oh-so-shiny wooden floor.

"Not at all," Alison said. "You got me out of that horrid contract with that scumbag Johannsson." She shuddered. "The way that creep *looked* at me."

"Never again, my dear," Petey Boy said. "And it didn't interfere with his debt to my partners at the Blue Dollar Club. Well done." His frown was nothing more than a slight crease between his eyebrows. "Though I suppose you ought to be compensated for your time, Mr. Genovese. I suppose your standard rate will do?"

"Keep it," I said, then shook my head. Directed my next words at Alison. "I've been wondering all day how anyone managed to get to the Mouse, but I'm looking at the reason, aren't I? Alison, Alison, Alison. You cozied up to him, then set him up so these two could eliminate Mariucci's power threat and give him a human sacrifice big enough to drag this lunk all the way to teak."

"Hey," Jake said. "I'm smarter than you, Carlo. I didn't just get played by a pair of green eyes."

"Your boss could offer a hundred souls to different Pagan gods in your name, Jake, and you'd still be a lunk."

Petey Boy frowned. "Mind your manners, Mr. Genovese. You are speaking to a Catholic."

"Oh, forget him," Alison said. "Let him crawl back under his rock. He can't hurt us."

Two doors leading into the back of Tony's place. And the moment Alison finished speaking, both of them burst open. I threw my hands out wide and fingers splayed even before the boys from Special Wands and Thaumaturgy started hollering commands.

Jake was stupid enough to start reaching for his wand. Eight blasts put him down so hard he'd need medical just to avoid a coma.

Petey Boy was smart enough to just put his hands up and close his mouth. Alison made the mistake of yelling threats at me. And every one of those threats would come back at her when her court day came.

The boys in blue had heard every word spoken in the back of Tony's, as of the moment I crushed the carnation they gave me. One of those last stops I'd made, and the one I had hoped wouldn't pan out.

I hadn't given the cops *everything* they'd need to put those three away, but I'd given them a good start. Made clear mention of human sacrifice, conspiracy to commit human sacrifice, murder with thaumaturgic intent, conspiracy to commit murder with thaumaturgic intent, and probably a couple of other things the D.A. could come up with. Metaphysical racketeering, maybe.

Alison, Petey Boy, and Jake had all taken their turns to speak, without anyone denying the charges. And with human sacrifice involved, that was enough for an arrest and to get warrants for the kind of thorough investigation that the D.A. could really sink her teeth into.

Might not stick to Petey Boy. Not with his clout. I'd have to watch myself for a while.

Jake, though. Going for his wand – teak, yet – against police orders would guarantee he'd be off the streets for a couple of years, at least. And it was going to make the rest of the charges look worse for him.

So Petey Boy lost *two* of his top killers this month. Gave me better odds, if Petey Boy beat the rap.

And Alison, well, she wasn't a succubus, but she might as well have had the horns, fangs and bat wings, far as I was concerned. Seeing her look that comfy with scum like Petey Boy Mariucci, that killed any feelings I had left for her.

Even if Alison beat the rap, she was out of my life for good.

SHADOW OF A CURSE

Adventure fantasy. I do so enjoy adventure fantasy. Reading it. Writing it. I'm not sure if that's the legacy of years of roleplaying games or some of my formational reading in adventure fantasy. Probably both.

This is one of my adventure fantasy stories, set in a world that – for some reason – I haven't returned to yet. I like the story and the setting, though, so I may write more stories in that world, at some point.

As a point of potential interest, the main character's style of magic is derived from the Old Norse concept of *seidh*, a type of witchcraft. Not so much in the way his magic works, but in the idea of him traveling from town to town, Seeing for people, casting spells and breaking curses.

I've taken a number of liberties with the concepts, of course.

APPLES WEREN'T SUPPOSED TO FLOAT IN THE AIR. EVERYONE KNEW THAT. If an apple slipped from the edge of a barmaid's tray, it was supposed to fall down to bounce on the weathered oak of the floor. It wasn't supposed to stop itself in mid-air, catching the immediate attention of a half-dozen of the tavern's revelers in the process.

It wasn't supposed to stop all conversation at the three nearest bench tables while mercenaries and tradesmen and farmers alike turned their attention to stare at the sweet green globe the size of a man's fist, twisting in the air limned in a golden sheen.

But the apple did just that. Perhaps the first time in the history of the Green Goose tavern that a single apple had drawn the attention of hungry men and women from their feast on the night's roast boar and snap peas, to say nothing of the mugs of fine beer forgotten in so many hands.

An apple floated in mid-air. Magic. More magic than most of them would see in a lifetime.

More magic than Asi should have spent for no better reason than to turn a pretty barmaid's expression from irritation to awestruck wonder. But only a year past his own apprenticeship, Asi still believed that wonder alone was worth the cost of a little magic.

And the barmaid was very pretty. Long black hair with the slight curve of an arrow's flight. That northern tilt to her brown eyes alongside the slender build of a woman who had never carried an axe. Her complexion a rich brown kissed by lemons rather than snowy, and her undyed cotton dress hung barely past her knees.

So different from the women of Asi's icy homeland.

Asi raised his gold-limned left hand and the apple lifted up through the air to float before the barmaid's face. She laughed with glee as she touched the apple. It fell into her hand as the sheen of gold vanished from around it and around Asi's hand. She smiled wide-eyed at Asi, and he shared that smile before the moment was ruined.

"Varlock."

Asi didn't see who spoke the title, but no sooner had someone uttered it than the word spread through the tavern like a hushed echo, with varying degrees of accent and inebriation. He was surprised they knew the word here, though perhaps they knew it only by rumor.

Dozens of eyes turned toward him. Most of them belonging to locals like the barmaid. Other eyes from wanderers and mercenaries and traders from the southern wastes or the western archipelago. Some of them reached for coin purses. Others narrowed their eyes in suspicion. But a few reached for weapons. Just in case.

Eight long bench tables in the room, all full, and all with attention turning Asi's way. He felt them scrutinize his frost-white skin and long, sun pale hair. Marks of his homeland as true as his gray wolf cloak or – apparently – the red shirt he wore with his leather trousers.

So much attention made him glance past the bench tables to the corners. Assessing the room again. Another round table in each corner, plus the two-countered bar running like a spike down the center, from the back of the common room to the mid-point. The doors into the kitchen were behind the bar. A large stone hearth in each long wall, and stairs at the back leading to rooms upstairs.

Asi sat alone at a round table. Near to the front door, but all the way across the tavern from those stairs. He had a room waiting for him, if he still got to use it. And he had yet to enjoy his own dinner.

With every eye in the tavern on him now, and his title on the lips of every patron, Asi admonished himself to leave the local women alone next time.

But then he thought of the barmaid's smile, and knew he would do the same thing the next time. And the time after that.

One of the locals was the first to gather his courage. An older man, in an undyed linen tunic and pants with a rope belt, which appeared to be the local fashion. He had the slight bow to his back that came from a life of field work, and a wispy white beard dripping down from his chin like a melting icicle.

"Varlock," he said, with a smoother bow than Asi expected. And his voice sounded strong, certain. Perhaps the local farmers did more talking than back home. "I—"

"Before you begin..." said Asi, holding up a hand, and the little old man stilled his mouth and waited patiently for Asi to speak. "I need you all to hear this. Those of my order are not 'for hire' like the kanuas of the archipelago or the sorcerers of the wastes. I am a varlock. I will sit and See for this town if you wish, but I must be fed and lodged by the town, and not my own coin. And each seeker will receive an answer only as fair and valuable as the offering made."

Formal phrasing, used by every varlock. Some assumed it meant only the rich could afford a Seeing. In truth, it meant the more personally important the question, the more personally important the offering must be to receive a meaningful answer.

"I am San," the old man said. "And I sit on the council for this, the township of Thir. And we do not need you to See for us, though of course we appreciate the offer."

Several in the crowd groaned at that and a few uttered protests, but not loudly. They must indeed have known the reputation of the varlocks, for they seemed to know that if a community leader said there would be no Seeing, no individual had the right to ask for one.

Perhaps a floating apple was not the most magic these locals would see in their lifetime after all.

"But we do have need of a varlock," San said loudly over the grumbles. "It is said that varlocks are curse breakers. And there is a curse on our lands."

Asi felt his stomach suggest that he was not so hungry as he'd thought. Why did he have to show off? He could have ridden out of this little town in the morning and never again given it a moment's thought. He would not have had to risk his life, his magic and at least one ninth part of his soul against the source of a land curse.

But then he looked at the barmaid and her evident interest in the mysterious varlock talking to a council member.

And Asi knew. He would do it again the same way the next time, assuming he survived.

After all, what was life without a little risk and the occasional interest of a pretty girl?

Asi invited San to join him at the table and San told the barmaid – whose name was Kyo – that the varlock's meal would be paid for by the town tonight, and that she should bring the best beer with dinner, and brandy with cherries and sweet apples for dessert.

Though they sat alone in the corner, Asi noticed that the rest of the tavern conversation had hushed, if not in fact lulled. It seemed that everyone was curious to listen in on what the councilor had to say. Curious enough that Asi could hear the fires on both sides of the room crackle and pop their spruce logs, and even the pouring of the master of the house at the bar.

Asi settled back into his simple chair and regarded San with raised eyebrows. The councilman smiled.

"This cannot be the first time you have discussed business in front of a crowd."

"It's the first time I've been in a town this small that knew the rules and expectations of dealing with varlocks." Asi tilted his head. "At least, a town that does not see snowfall for at least half the year."

"There is a tall woman who comes through once a year and Sees for us. She stands about your height with hair as red as sunset. She wears a gray wolf cloak the twin of yours."

"Rika?" Asi sat forward, both elbows on the rough wood of the table and his entire attention on San, who seemed pleased that Asi knew the name. "*Rika* has Seen for you?"

"She has done other things for us as well."

Beneath his breath, Asi uttered a small prayer of thanks that San had refused a Seeing. If Rika was all they knew of varlocks here, they would have very high expectations for Asi's work...

San smiled, and relaxation seemed to spread from the old man's eyes down his beard and all through his body.

"Good," said San. "Humility. I wondered."

Humility. Asi almost laughed. Saying his own power was nothing to Rika's was like saying a snowball was nothing to an avalanche.

"If Rika can't break the curse—"

"She has not been here since the curse was laid, and if we wait for her we will all be dead before she arrives."

"All of you?" Asi sat back in his chair, so struck by the councilman's statement that he failed to give Kyo so much as a flirtatious look when she filled his mug with beer. "But most curses affect one person. One family. One farm. One business. That is their nature."

"And we are one town." San shrugged. "One town with our cattle and sheep dying and our horses dead already. One town paying foreign hunters to kill boars while we fight to save our livestock. I don't know how we have angered such a powerful witch, but we have. And she blames the whole of our community."

Asi shook his head.

"No witch could do this. A varlock could do it, if powerful enough..." Asi closed his eyes. "You swear to me on your town's children that you have not angered Rika?"

"I swear to you on our children and on the children I hope they live to bear, here in Thir we treat Rika as a treasured aunt. No door is closed to her. No meal or bed denied her. Offerings left for her when she is not looking. Her money spurned when offered. Our people would shed their blood for her."

Asi nodded slowly. If he had any lingering doubts, those words assuaged them. The goal of a varlock was not power or glory, but community. That Rika came through annually, and that Thir treated her properly, meant that this was not merely someplace Rika came to See. This was a place she could call home. And no other varlock would *dare* to curse a place *Rika* called home.

Yet something had. Something that could spread a curse past the bonds of family and property to community itself. And if not a varlock, then that meant more power than anything Asi had faced before.

Fear twitched in his stomach, clenched someplace lower. This was Asi's first trip down from the frozen east. He wished to do nothing more than ride for the coast and visit the archipelago, where the sea was said to flow as warm as blood and they shared fruits the like of which Asi had never tasted.

But this was a community in crisis. And though the source of such a curse may well have been beyond his means to defeat, Asi could no more walk away from their troubles than he could fail to return each year to the village that bore him, and treat its woes.

And so Asi swallowed a sigh and said the formal words of a varlock to a community leader he is promising to aid.

"I am sorry to hear of your troubles, uncle. Tell me everything so I know how to help."

San leaned forward and clasped Asi's hand. And then he told the tale. Others from nearby tables stood to offer insights and other viewpoints. Some of the wanderers left, uncomfortable, as the locals laid bare their troubles. And Asi was certain he could see some of the merchants and traders looking for angles to improve their profits.

That was reason enough to interrupt the tales of cows and sheep wasting away even as they ate and drank their normal share of fodder and water. Of pear trees stunting at the blossom, and the apple and cherry trees that seemed to be following suit. Of farmland that drank deep the rains, yet thirsted for more.

Asi stood amid the recitations, stopping a farmer mid-sentence.

"A warning," Asi said, "to those who trade and sell. Rika may not be here, but I am varlock enough to deal with any who would exploit this curse. Do *not* let me hear of raised prices or unreasonable demands."

And ignoring the grumbles and furtive looks among merchants and mercenaries, Asi sat and listened to every one of the complaints while the problem grew and grew in his own mind. Curses dealt with health, or livestock, or crops, or land. They did not deal with health *and* livestock *and* crops *and* land. Not even a varlock's curse did so many things at once. A varlock's curse would pick a single path to cut through a community and slice it to ribbons in a fortnight.

But this was different. This was slow, thorough, and ugly.

And Asi had no idea what was causing it.

Asi woke in the morning on the innkeeper's finest feather bed, entwined in the limbs of Kyo. He kissed her as she awoke, tender, to savor her sweetness just a little longer before going out to face this town's need.

Kyo made a small sound, squeezed her eyes closed, and tried to pull him back down to sleep. But much as he might have desired to join her, Asi could not permit that. If he lay back down with Kyo, he knew he would not leave that bed until the sun was high in the sky, and he needed to see the afflicted area by the first rays of the dawn.

So he kissed her again, and he stroked her cheek to soothe her. And once her brown eyes had fluttered closed and her breaths grown deeper, Asi leaned down to enjoy her warm scent that reminded him of nutmeg.

Then he placed his hand on the center of her naked chest, and muttered a half-Seeing, half-blessing.

"When the rays of the longest day begin to fade, they shall shine last upon he who is your truest love. You shall see that truth in one another's eyes, and shall be happy together through all the trials of life."

And just for a moment, a reddish glow flowed from Asi's chest and down his arm to spread across Kyo's body. When it faded, she smiled in her sleep.

The night before Kyo might been willing to share Asi's bed anyway, because he was handsome and mysterious. But once Asi agreed to aid the community of Thir with all his skill as a varlock, no bed would be denied him and he would leave every lover blessed.

Asi left his cloak behind in the room, and donned a shirt of sky blue over his leather pants and heavy leather boots. He broke his fast on the apple and small wedge of sharp yellow cheese that had been left on a plate for him, and examined the town in the pre-dawn as he walked north along the smooth main road toward the first farm harmed by the curse.

Rika must have been coming here for years. Asi could see the signs of a strong community. A community that helped its own.

The houses all began small, but steady, and spaced widely enough to expand back and out as families grew. And every house in the town itself looked solid. Good woods in the construction and sealed against rain, trued angles, and shingled roofs. No family had suffered because of a father or mother's poor fortune or ineptitude with a hammer.

Even now he could hear the families rising to begin their days. Calling to each other, or to their livestock. Those latter cries sounding plaintive in Asi's ears, as though they hoped to persuade their animals to live through the sheer power of love and need.

Multiple wells. Large in the center of town, and smaller secondary wells spaced every few hundred steps. This was a community that pulled together despite a gentle climate and forgiving soil that made all too many communities selfish.

No wonder Rika felt home here.

As Asi reached the farms north of town, he saw that the family markings here and there on the fences had been redone two or three times. Territory disputes at the edge of town? Interesting. Perhaps Thir was not so harmonious as Asi had thought.

Asi considered that as he reached the Etu farm, the farthest out from town center. If this town's harmony had begun to fray at the edges, then along the edges Asi might find the answers to this curse.

If so, this was where he would learn the truth.

Asi took up the proper position, right knee pressed against the earth just outside the fence of the Etu farm. Back straight and eyes level with the distant mountains of the horizon. Right hand out to the side, palm up. Left hand out to the side, palm down.

In the language of his homeland, he chanted, "Far Farer grant me a grain of your Sight. Show me what hides between darkness and light."

The first ray of sunshine crested the mountain peaks and shone down across the valley onto the farm.

Asi saw the land cracked drier than the southern sandy wastes. He saw desperate carrion birds squabbling over the scraps of corpses too desiccated to feed even one of them. Buildings fallen. Crops blackened.

Asi saw a land drained dry of life.

Then the moment passed, and Asi saw the Etu farm as it was rather than as it would be. Sickened, not dead. Not yet.

But one element still remained from what the Far Farer showed Asi. A wispy trail like a hint of black smoke, trailing north of town toward a dense forest a half-day distant.

Asi would need his horse.

***

ASI WAS OBLIGED TO REFUSE HELP THREE TIMES BEFORE THE TOWNSFOLK would let him ride forth alone to deal with the threat. They were strong men and women, and many of them had fought in defense of their own before. Some could even wield a sword as handily as an axe or hoe.

But Asi knew they would be useless against the thing that had cursed their town. True, weapons might have been able to harm, or even defeat it. Asi would not know that for certain until he traced that smoky trail to its source and determined exactly what manner of threat he faced.

But even if they could kill it, they would not be able to help Asi. Worse, they might hinder his progress. Some curses could only be broken while the curser lived. Killing the curser merely ensured that the spell ran its course.

The ways and varieties of magic were many, and no one, not even Rika, could claim to know them all. It was the calling of the varlock to puzzle through their secrets in service to others. So he accepted the one thing he needed – a scrap of parchment bearing the council's seal – and rode off on his own to face the threat.

To reach the thick, supposedly uninhabited forest, Asi had to leave the road where it bent west. The road would wind its way across the river Shem, heading for the nearest city. Or at least the nearest lord. Whichever way the locals ran things.

But even without a boundary marker, Asi knew the moment his chestnut palomino Ulf passed beyond the northern edge of the Etu farm. Yellowing grass grew greener, had more spring to it. The soil beneath was richer, darker, even softer than the hardening dryness of the farmlands behind him. The air smelled sweeter here, fresher. As though rain had been no more than three days past. The heat of the morning sunlight felt heartening on Asi's skin, rather than suggesting an itch that could not *quite* be felt.

Ulf's steps lightened as well, as though merely passing through Thir had weighed on the poor horse.

And so Asi spurred Ulf to a swift trot, determined to enter the distant forest before the sun reached its apex.

He reached the outlying ash trees perhaps an hour before high sun.

Asi dismounted, and stood before Ulf. He stroked the horse's blond mane, and spoke into his soft brown eyes. "Await me here, my friend. If you must flee a threat, follow the road west. I will find you. Do not return to Thir without me."

Asi sighed. "If I do not return by nightfall, go home."

A varlock's horse returning without the varlock was rare, and always merited investigation. If Asi died today, Ulf would carry the warning. Another would return to finish what Asi started. Perhaps Rika herself.

Ulf neighed an objection.

"Very well then," said Asi. "Dawn." Asi held up a warning finger. "I mean it. If I do not return by dawn, consider me lost. Do not tarry in danger, my friend."

Ulf snorted and jerked his head away. He took three firm steps along the tree line, glanced back at Asi, then pointedly began munching on grass.

"I don't like it either," said Asi. "But there are no roads through this forest, and I won't have you breaking an ankle. I'll be back by dawn, if I return at all."

Ulf munched some more grass, which was about all the agreement Asi could expect.

Asi turned back to the forest. He plucked three leaves from the nearest ash tree and one leaf from each of three small plants that formed the underbrush. He rooted around in the bushes, and among the twigs and fallen leaves until he had a feather from one of the local jays – blue – and a tuft of red fox fur.

He gathered all these things in his left hand, placed his right hand over them, not touching. Blue power flared from his solar plexus, then up his chest and down his arms to coalesce in his hands, lighting his gathered materials.

In the tongue of his native land, he whispered, "Wights and spirits, hear me. You who grow, who run, who fly. You who form this place, and you who call it home. Hear me. You who bear no evil, hear me. I seek a shadow hiding among you. I seek a darkness that poisons the land. I seek a foulness that corrodes animal and human alike. Let me be as one of you, for a time. Let me hunt as one of you, for a time. Let me call this place home, for a time. Help me root out this foulness, and I shall leave your home a better place than I found it."

The blue power faded. Asi moved his right hand aside. The leaves, the feather and the fur were gone from his left hand. In their place lay a single green feather, small and simple as the pinion of a sparrow.

Asi raised the feather reverently and whispered, "Thank you."

He placed the feather behind his right ear and started into the forest.

It was as though the forest opened wide before him. Every sight, every sound, every smell came to him, but all came filtered. The trees and underbrush were as background to the smoky trail he followed. He heard the birdsong, the chatter of squirrels, the cracking and rustling of countless animals going about their business, unconcerned about the human who was – for a time – as one of them. But those sounds were muffled as his ears strained for the unnatural, although, as yet, he heard nothing.

And the smells of the forest, the musk of the animals and the damp decay of recent rain, those hung back as well. No more prominent than his tongue's memory of the apples and sharp yellow cheese, eaten hours ago.

Overriding all these things, Asi could smell a whiff of corruption.

As of a wound that had begun to fester, but not yet gained the sickly sweetness of gangrene.

Only a hint, but it lay in the same direction as the smoky trail led him.

Surefooted and confident as any woodland creature, Asi began to run.

———

THE TRAIL LED ASI DEEP INTO THE FOREST. HE CROSSED SMALL HILLS and leapt creeks and streams, while all around him animals went about their day, unconcerned about his presence. If only he could have spared the attention to revel in this harmony. But he kept his focus on the thin, smoky trail, and on the thing that was cursing the township of Thir.

Between trees he followed it. Through bushes and across ditches, his attention never flagging.

Finally, the smoky trail dipped down to a pool.

The pool wasn't in a clearing. Ashes and beeches grew right up to its edge, and Asi could see their roots and underbrush dipping down as though expecting solid ground. Above, the canopy grew thick, and if the forest had not welcomed Asi, his eyes would have seen little. If anything.

But the forest did welcome Asi after his petition, and Asi could see the chunk of granite overhanging the pool, like a great gray diver preparing to plunge. It stood taller than Asi, and wider than a cart.

Asi could also see that this pool wasn't fed by streams. Nor rainwater, not under so thick a canopy. If the pool, itself, were natural, it would have to have been fed by an underground spring.

But this pool wasn't natural. No animals came here to drink. Asi could see no tracks, smell no spoor nor musk. In fact, he smelled little except for the rank corruption, strong enough now to turn his stomach and threaten to bring back up that sharp yellow cheese.

Asi pulled out the scrap of parchment bearing the seal of the council. He held it high, and a golden glow of power limned himself and the parchment as he spoke.

"I have come. I name myself protector of Thir. I name myself guardian of this forest. I name myself breaker of your curse. My name is Asi Kholsson, and I have come. Step forth and give answer."

The rock began to shift and bend, and beneath it the pool rushed up in a pillar of water. Rock flowed as though molten and began to twist and dance with the water, swirling together. Spiraling up, up, up all the way to the canopy some two dozen feet overhead, before crashing back down into a single shape.

A gray stone serpent, with watery blue eyes that rippled. Its body was thicker than Ulf, and long as one of the trees around it. The serpent coiled where the pool had been, head weaving back and forth, high in the air, as its hood flared out. Stone fangs glistened with water or poison.

Poison. Of course.

"What are you?" said Asi. This creature was like nothing they had back home.

"Varrr-loch," it rasped, and for a horrible moment Asi thought it was saying that it was once a varlock. But as it continued, Asi realized it was addressing him by a title he never gave it. Fortunately, it's voice became easier to understand as it continued. "Deny Thir. It is dead already. Leave this place. And live."

"If you know I am a varlock," said Asi, tucking the parchment back into his belt, "you know I won't. You *do* know of varlocks, don't you? That's why you act now. You fear Rika."

"You are no Rika."

"No, but that does tell me you can be killed." Asi smiled. "Break your curse and leave. Do these things and you will live."

Something that big should not have been fast.

It struck. Great dripping fangs plunged for Asi's chest.

Asi grabbed the stone mouth. Held it wide open, while the mouth bore him down. Onto his back among the twigs and fallen leaves.

Breath like rotted meat, practically a poison of its own. But the inside of the mouth was stone, not meat. No proper gullet then.

And that gave Asi an idea.

First, he channeled his connection to Thir into a golden glow of power and spent that glow in a single kick. He snapped off one of those poison fangs. Sent it flying.

The creature roared anger and pain. Pulled back for another strike.

Asi dove into the mouth. Beside the snapping fang he went, straight down the creature's throat. He could feel it rising high. Maybe trying to swallow. Maybe trying to expel him. But a creature that does not eat cannot really...

The inside of its throat began to shift. Grew slippery. Oily. Began to slide Asi down toward its center. Asi knew what would follow then. Another shift of shape, and then it would begin to crush him as surely as any digestive tract.

But Asi never planned on giving it the chance.

Green power spread from Asi's heart to envelope him, shining out into the glittery throat of the creature. "Thunderer, hear me. Defender of man. Smiter of monsters. Aid me now."

The throat shifted from a tube to a sphere. A tight sphere, growing tighter all the time.

"In the beginning the monsters ran wild," Asi prayed, "and only Your divine hand preserved us. I follow in your wake."

The sphere crunched in. Cutting off Asi's air. Squeezing him until his bones began to grind. His heart pounded as though it could beat its way out through the creature. His lungs desperately seized for air that wasn't there for them.

But Asi's mind was deep in prayer. Still his lips moved as the green glow around him grew brighter. And soundlessly he said *Like You, I bind communities together. Like you, I stand against the monsters. Aid me now. Not for me, but for Thir.*

And somewhere in the skies above, the Thunderer heard him.

Within the belly of the beast, where no sound should reach, Asi heard a clap of thunder. And the moment he did, he threw every drop of power he could summon against the beast. Green fire exploding outward while the crack of thunder came down from above.

The sphere froze. Then cracked. Then split in half, dropping Asi on blackened, ruined ground as the two half of a gray granite egg rocked slowly to a stop.

Asi crawled forward until he could lay on good, healthy dirt, and collapsed. Panting gratefully for every lungful of air. His heart lurching, as though it couldn't quite believe it was still beating, and half-wanted to beat fast for the joy of it and half-wanted to slow to a speed that ensured it wouldn't burst.

It did slow, eventually. And his breaths came back at a more normal pace as well.

And finally, Asi was able to roll to his feet. He brushed leaves from his long blond hair, but did not concern himself with the ones stuck to his blue shirt or brown leather pants, much less sticking out of his heavy leather boots.

He forced himself to cross the blackened patch of dirt to find the broken, poisoned fang.

Asi gathered leaves and wove a quick pad he could use to pick up the fang without touching the poison. The poison would accumulate on the leaves, but that was well enough.

He would need that poison, and the fang, for the hardest part of this venture: breaking the curse.

And with that, Asi started back for Ulf, and then Thir.

As Asi rode back into town, shortly after dusk, he noted the territory marks around the Etu farm, and the surrounding farms. Especially which nearby farmer most recently seemed to claim land that had once belonged to the Etu family.

But he did not stop to deal with that. Not now.

The curse had to come first. If Asi could not break the curse, the rest ... would not matter.

Still carrying the poison fang in his hands, he rode for the center of town. It's heart. In some places it would be marked by a statue, or by the house of the founder, or perhaps the mayor.

Here in Thir, the center of town was a marketplace, all but abandoned right now. Dust and dry dirt, not even any stiff yellow grass grew here.

Only one stall was set up, and Asi could tell at a glance that it was the stall of a traveling merchant. None of the locals had enough food to sell. His stomach growled at the scent of roast chicken.

Asi noted to himself to make sure that merchant was charging a fair price. Yet one more thing to deal with, once the curse was dealt with.

Townsfolk gathered around the edges of the marketplace, but came no closer. Either fearful or respectful. The merchant began closing up shop immediately.

"You," called Asi to the merchant. "If you have been cheating these people, I will find you."

The merchant didn't answer. Only smiled and nodded as though he did not speak the local language. Asi noted the bald patch among the thatch of black hair atop his tanned scalp. Noted the wrinkles and graying whiskers. Noted the silks of his clothes, and the farmhouse drawing on his wagon.

Yes, if Asi needed to, he could find this one again.

But first, the curse.

Asi slid from his saddle in the very center of the marketplace. Ulf, having seen Asi break curses before, wisely trotted off to join the crowd at the edge of the marketplace. Although, at least, Ulf did give Asi worried glances.

At least someone would mourn him, if this did not work.

Asi lay the sopping woven pad on the ground before him, the broken fang atop it.

Asi took his two fingers of his right hand and drew a circle in the dirt around the pad. Then another, larger, around that.

Asi sat cross-legged in the outer circle.

He slammed his fist down in the dust, and a violet light flared out of him to burn like fire along the edges of both circles.

And then Asi's body slumped in place as his spirit reached past his physical confines for the spirit of the fang. While Asi's spirit looked much as his body did, down to the color of his shirt, the spirit of the fang was the whole of the granite serpent done in miniature, hissing at Asi as though laughing.

Asi grabbed the serpent in both hands.

"Fell creature," he said. "You are spent. Deceased. Nothing."

"But I *am*," it interrupted.

Asi continued the formal words of challenge to a curse spirit. "But connected to you is the curse on this land. I claim this curse is broken. I claim this curse is done. I claim this curse is over. Deny my words if you dare."

The miniature version of that great serpent – no larger now than a modest-sized garter snake – opened its mouth wide. Out poured a stream of sickly green smoke. Washing over Asi. Eating slowly away at his spirit. Burning pain spread throughout him, everywhere the smoke touched. So terrific was the pain that he could feel it reach through to his body, making it twitch and foam purple at the mouth. He could feel it trying to dry him out and force him to decay, as it had the lands and the animals of the people of Thir.

Asi reached into his core to the fire that burned at the heart of the nine parts of his spirit. One part for each of the nine worlds. One part for each of the nine tasks set before each human being, before the gates of the afterworld would swing wide to admit him after death.

And Asi met that poisonous cloud of curse with the fire of his essence.

Most curses did not require such measures. Many were little more than spells that could be unwoven or countered, with a little time and study. But this was a greater curse than any Asi had faced before. And he knew his only chance was to match power against power.

The poisonous cloud burned at him, even as the fire of his essence burned at it.

Asi held nothing back. He let his mind go blank. Forsook thoughts of home, of comfort, of the archipelago he hoped to see – everything that was for himself, Asi set aside.

He focused only on the need. On the good people of Thir. People who dug more wells than they needed, so none would have to carry water farther than they had to. Who helped each other build, and reap, and shared in such prosperity as they managed.

These people mattered. Not Asi. Not now.

And so, with all thoughts of self out of the way, the fire within Asi's soul burned hotter still. Burned away the smoke that scalded him. Burned away the sliver of serpent spirit that clung to the curse on this town.

Burned the curse itself down to ash, and that ash to nothing at all.

But such power is not tapped without price. And the moment the last of the curse burned away, Asi fell back into his body. Or rather, less of Asi fell back into his body than left it.

A ninth part of Asi's soul hovered on the brink of death. A cold pain, and a darkness that sucked Asi down.

ASI WOKE, WHICH WAS MORE THAN HE EXPECTED. HE ACHED everywhere, even in places he hadn't known he could ache. Each beat of his heart, each slow, shallow breath, each blink of his eyes – it seemed that even things his body did without his intention carried aches.

At least he was laying on something soft. Had to be a mattress. Felt like a featherbed. Was he back in that room in the tavern, where he had lain with Kyo what seemed like a lifetime ago?

His mouth was dry, but tasted vaguely of chicken broth. He expected to smell himself. Old sweat or worse. But he didn't, which meant someone had washed him. And he could smell beeswax, which was what made him realize he could see. A dim light – still too bright right now – from two candles on the table beside him. One green, one blue.

Beeswax? Green and blue?

Asi's very eye sockets complained when he narrowed his eyes and forced them to focus on those candles. They glistened, as though oiled...

Asi sniffed the air again, checking for...there it was. Pine resin and camphor.

But who would know to—

The door opened, and Asi's beleaguered mind realized three things at the same time.

First, he was in a room with a door.

Second, this was, in fact, the room he had stayed in with Kyo.

Third, Rika had just entered the room.

She looked like the great Vana-goddess herself. Tall and fire-haired, with curves even her wolf skin cloak could not hide. Asi had seen her before, yes, at the triennial gathering, but never so close. She seemed too big for the room, as though her power pressed out upon the wooden walls and even on Asi's lungs and mouth.

At least, Asi liked to think that was the reason his breath caught.

Rika smiled, warm and welcoming as a hearth fire.

"Good," she said, "you're awake. I'd hoped to speak to you before I left."

"Left?" Asi croaked, then cleared his throat until Rika poured water from a wooden pitcher into a wooden cup, and handed him the cup. Two swallows later, he could form words.

"How long have you been here?"

"Three days." She nodded. "Long enough to ensure that Thir was doing what needed to be done for you." She smiled. "They have tended you as one of their own."

"You taught them well," Asi said, automatically, while the meaning of her words crept through his head. If they cared for him with love...

"Yes," Rika said, no doubt seeing realization spread across his face. "That ninth part of your soul is healing. Another moon and you'll be yourself again."

"*Another* moon?"

"Oh yes. You've been unconscious for some time."

"But the Etu. Their neighbors."

"Witches," said Rika. "Who made a pact with something bigger than themselves. I know. They fled the moment they were free to. The moment you broke the curse." Her expression darkened like an ice storm at sea. "I'm setting out for them now."

Asi tried to sit up, but though his neck made the effort, his torso refused to assist. He fell back into bed.

"No," said Rika. "Let me do this. Thir has been my home longer than it has been yours. Besides," – she smiled – "you've already done the hard part."

She left then, and Asi sank back into bed while he considered what Rika just said. *His home.* Thir, who had known the work of only Rika before him, now welcomed Asi as one of them. This was his home now. The first home he had made for himself outside his icy homeland.

More than he had ever dreamed of accomplishing on this trip.

The door opened again. Kyo, in her undyed cotton dress, with a smile and a bowl of soup.

"Ready to eat?" she said, and the fondness in her eye was something Asi had only ever seen back in the cold east. At the towns he had visited, Seen for, aided regularly.

To see that look here, in a place he had only been stopping on his way west, warmed him to the very core.

"Yes," he said. "Yes I am. And thank you."

THE TRIALS OF REBIRTH

Speaking of *seidh*, the ritual the main character performs in this story derives from an actual *seidh* ritual performed in this world.

Back when I was in college – and shortly after I graduated – every so often someone would ask about what I'd do with a degree in Religious Studies, with a double emphasis in Mythology and Ritual.

The true answer is that I write stories like this one.

Elements of myth are part and parcel to who we are as human beings. They're universal. And I do enjoy writing about them from time to time.

Oh, and if you ever try *Utiseta*, I make no promises about, nor take any responsibility for, what may or may not happen. This story may have a basis in the myths and rituals of this world, but remember, it's *fiction*.

(The preceding paragraph brought to you by my having been raised by lawyers.)

It wasn't much of a mountain peak, but it wasn't much of a life I was leaving behind.

Tucked in amid the redwoods and sequoias of a California state park, I'd found a peak called … well, I don't think it had a proper name. Let's just call it Mount Dagny. It was a rocky outjut that probably wasn't tall enough to satisfy geologists who might want to get technical about what really constituted a mountain.

But it was just right for the new beginning I needed.

All around Mount Dagny were little slopes of dry dirt and underbrush that might serve as hills, comparatively speaking. Little wannabe hills, where the trees grew stunted as my life, because the rocky ground beneath them wasn't fertile enough.

And there in the center, Mount Dagny itself stuck up like a middle finger aimed squarely at dissenters.

Perfect.

I'd been hiking all day in the August heat when I found my little mountain. Mind you, August heat in Northern California was more like early spring heat down in Arizona, where I'd finished my graduate work only two years prior. So I still had two full canteens of water hanging from my belt, and my cargo shorts and tee shirt smelled more of trail dirt than my own dried sweat. Hell, even the socks inside my hiking boots felt dry instead of sweat-soaked.

Truth was, I'd almost given up hope. Well, in more than one way, really, but I mean that day of hiking, I'd almost despaired of finding the kind of place I needed. The late afternoon sky was already burning its way from blue to orange, starting from the west, and I was on the brink of heading back to my car with one more failure under my belt.

Heck, I'd already started rehearsing my excuses to the rangers for only having a day pass, but getting back to the parking lot after dark by the light of my brighter-than-I-kept-expecting L.E.D. flashlight.

But then I spotted my little Mount Dagny, and I knew I'd found the right place. I knew there was no turning back. Not now. I got that little buzz of adrenaline going, felt the good kind of jitters in my joints. Knew that buzz would give my fingers a little extra grip on the ascent, would tighten my legs just a little more when I needed extra.

And I'd need a little extra, going up. Gray and rocky my little mountain looked, by the growing shadows of early sunset, with a peak too narrow for me to lie down on.

Not that I intended to lie down.

A quick check of the broad trail told me I had the place to myself. Confirmed what I'd already figured. Just me and the occasional singing bird or barking squirrel. I hadn't spotted another hiker in at least half an hour. Most of the people still in the park had probably already set up their tents and built their fires in their little reserved clearings. Some of them likely had tins of stew going, or hot dogs roasting, or even just marshmallows on sticks for the traditional smores.

My stomach rumbled at that thought. I don't even think I'd touched my rations, which were the half dozen grainy "chocolate" meal bars I'd stuffed into my pockets, just in case. Not much, but I could never stomach trail mix, and I didn't like the way sandwiches got mushed up in my pockets during a day of hiking.

Meal bars weren't much more appetizing than a smushed sandwich, but that was just as well. Might help keep me on point when my stomach started rumbling louder and louder until it finally rivaled the engine of a D.C. 10.

No food for me. Not until sunrise. Not now that I'd found my little mountain.

I checked over my shoulders once more, but apart from a little rustling bush to one side of the trail, nothing.

Confident that it was just me, I knelt at the foot of little Mount Dagny, my knees grinding a little into the harsh dirt. I tucked my boots under my butt. Put my hands on my thighs, and straightened my back so I sat tall and true. Eyes closed. Slow, deep breaths, the kind that flared my nostrils wide only a moment before doing the same to my lungs and diaphragm.

About two dozen breaths like that, steadying myself until I could hear the breeze rustling the redwood needles. Until I could feel that gentle breeze kissing my cheeks and forehead, rustling my short brown hair. Until my skin balanced the cooling temperature to a point moderate enough to ignore.

No incantation. Not for this part. This wasn't really the beginning. Ritually speaking, this was prologue. Attuning myself to the land and the mountain and the rising night. The rite itself couldn't properly begin until I reached the peak. But this first step, without it, the rest would have meant nothing. Would have made the ascent no more meaningful than my day's hike.

So I sat and breathed until I felt myself part of the evening air, part of the dirt, part even of the tiny mountain before me.

And then I started to climb.

I REACHED THE BARE ROCK OF THE PEAK WHILE HALF OF THE SUN STILL poked its face above the sea of trees that formed my horizon. I was sweating now, shivering a bit in the cooler air at this modest elevation.

Irritating. A delay. I was too much in my body now, and not enough part of the land around me.

I had to sit – cross-legged this time on the cool gray rock of the peak – and flare more deep breaths until I shunted away the remains of my adrenaline. Until my muscles stopped shivering from cold or twitching from the effort of my free-climb. Until my complaining belly stopped asking for a grainy "chocolate" meal bar.

Settled myself back into the evening. Connecting to the peak, as well as to the oncoming night.

I finished before the sun vanished over the horizon. A bare sliver remained, but enough. Enough to still caress me with the last light of day, before I began my *utiseta*.

Utiseta, the way my father explained it to me, literally meant "sitting out," but it was so much more than those two words made it sound. *Utiseta* was a way to connect with the world so that I could slip through the morass into the truth that lay beneath. To align the nine parts of my soul, and open up possibilities that the working day denied me.

Had I been a *seidhmadhr* like my grandfather, I could have performed a great many wonders while sitting out. Found my *fylgia*, my animal spirit, which I could have sent forth to spy on distant places, or work my will. Sent my soul traveling the great world ash *Yggdrasil*, for knowledge from the dead, or perhaps from the *alfs*. Blessed my friends and family. Cursed my enemies. That sort of thing.

Alas, I never had that much talent, and my dear grandfather was dead. I only hoped I had enough of his gift inside me to change my life this once.

The sun slipped at last below the horizon. And I began to sing.

The syllables were my approximations of the words of ancient Norse. My best phonetic estimates. But in my heart and in my head rang the meaning I sang into them: *Freyja, fairest of the Vanir, bearer of the Brising necklace, mistress of Seidh. It is I, Erik Nilsson, who calls you. Son of a son of one your great* seidhmadhr *Lars Nilsson. Fare forth falcon-formed to guide me this night, for my soul is burdened by failures. All about me turns to ash. Only you can bear me up again.*

I don't know how many times I sang. I kept singing until my voice got rough. Until even through my connection I could feel the rising chill of night, and the hints of cramps in my legs, the taste of trail dust on my tongue. The burden of my body, trying to distract me from my goal.

But I sang on. On until I heard the sign I'd awaited.

The rush and flap of falcon wings.

Freyja had heard me. Freyja would help me. I could be born again.

If I could survive the trials of rebirth.

Somewhere, my body sat on that little excuse for a mountain. Below me? Behind me? I didn't know. But my soul – or at least a ninth part of my soul, I'd never been too clear on the theology of it – was walking along a dirt path.

I was still wearing hiking boots and cargo shorts, with canteens dangling from my belt. Or at least I seemed to be. Just as the cloudless sky above me seemed a bright, pale blue. But the sun, the sun was unlike anything I'd ever seen before. Oh, it was still a great ball of yellow flame, but in this place it rested in a chariot that was pulled through the sky by two horses. And behind it came a great slavering wolf, chasing as fast as its legs would carry it.

The wolf's name I remembered from my grandfather's stories: Sköll. But the horses and the charioteer, those I couldn't remember.

The world around my dirt path just looked like, well, the world I was used to, if nothing like the park my body sat in. High, snow-crested mountain peaks to my left and right, while my path led me through what looked like a lush valley. Forests of oak trees, and rolling hills of green grass. The only thing that looked out of place, well, was the dirt path.

It looked ... fresh. It even smelled of recently turned earth, not at all packed down by centuries of marching feet, the way I would have expected in a place like this.

I couldn't hear Freyja's wings now. Not here. Which meant anytime now I could expect...

Suddenly the path was blocked. One moment it had spread out before me, clear as the blue sky above, and now a man stood in the center of it, barring my way.

He had the wrinkles and gray hair to be sixty, but he looked fit inside his gray pinstripe suit, and his ice blue eyes issued the challenge of a much younger man.

"Where do you think you're going?" His voice was soft, but menacing.

I thought about trying to step around him. Goodness knew there was plenty of grass on either side, but as I started to take a step, I heard the clacking of a falcon's beak.

Around was not an option.

"My path lies this way," I said. "Please move."

"My bank invested a great deal in you. You go nowhere until you pay your debt to me."

"My business collapsed. As I told your real-world counterparts, I don't have your money. What I did have, you already claimed when I filed for bankruptcy. There's nothing more. Now—"

"It's not enough."

"There's nothing else!"

"Then go back."

I tried to slip past him then, but he was faster. If I cut right, he was there. If I cut left, he was there. I already knew that stepping off the path was failure.

I tried to hit him. It was all I could think of.

He blocked my punch and hit me in the chest so hard I flew backwards and landed on my butt.

But the punch didn't hurt. And the landing didn't hurt. I felt them, but there was no sharpness or pressure to them.

I couldn't fight him. But I had nothing to give him except...

I stripped off my shirt.

"Here. I'm giving you the shirt off my back."

The banker took the shirt. But instead of stepping aside, he held out his hand.

With a sigh, I stripped naked and handed him the rest of my clothes. Really, the rest of the worldly possessions that I had in this place.

The banker stepped aside.

I took three steps before I heard the rustle of Freyja's wings and she bore me to another place.

METAPHOR. I MIGHT HAVE BEEN A LITTLE HAZY ON THE THEOLOGY OF what was happening, but metaphor I understood.

The banker had taught me how the game worked. So as I faced each trial, their solutions came to me quickly now.

My black lab, Strider, who died last month because I couldn't afford the operation to save him when his belly got twisted. I cried just seeing him there in the road before me, solemn instead of happy. To him I gave my heart without hesitation, and he licked my face before I moved on.

The children who showed up next confused me. Twelve of them, the oldest only barely toddlers. I couldn't puzzle through the block they represented, until I realized that each of them had some feature that was plainly my own. Some my blue eyes, others my fine hair, still others my dimpled chin. Then the ages made sense. These were all children born from the sperm I'd sold for pocket money in college. Children who shared my genes, but no other connection to my family. Parts of myself that I hadn't known existed.

To them I offered the parts that contributed to their birth.

My professors were a surprise. Six of them, from both my undergrad and graduate studies. They clamored over who had the greatest claim on me, but I couldn't figure out what they represented until I remembered that each had written glowing letters of recommendation for me. To graduate school, to scholarships, to internships. All of them had spoken for me. So to them I gave my voice.

My college friends arrived in a pack, as unhappy to see me here as they'd been in the regular world where they'd stopped returning my calls. They made it clear that they were tired of never hearing good news from me. So to them I gave my ears.

My ex-girlfriend Tina was next. Beautiful red-haired Tina, whose own beauty salon weathered the changing economy so much better than I had with my ill-timed wholesale business. Tina had left me because she saw no future with me. I offered her my eyes.

I knew my mother by her touch. Her gentle stroke of my forehead, followed by my father's firm handshake, and my brother's pale imitation. I could feel the rest of my relatives queued up to shake my hand or kiss my cheek. Cousins and aunts and uncles, perhaps even generations of family going back to the days of the long ships and before. They were my family. They were what held me together. So to them I gave my skin.

By that point, I kept expecting I had to come to the end. I'd started feeling surprised every time I felt the rush of Freyja's flapping wings. But that was foolish on my part. I should have known. Nine worlds, nine parts to the soul, nine trials for rebirth.

And at that point, I'd only had seven.

I was getting a little worried though. I was just about out of me, and I wasn't sure how I'd be able to tell what my final trials were. I'd been a little too hasty handing out my senses.

So when the tap on my forehead stopped me, I tried to ask who it was but I'd already given away my voice. I did the only thing I could think of. I shrugged.

A hand grasped my right hand. Shook it once, then shifted grips in a pattern I knew well and instantly matched. The six-gripped handshake that ended with linked thumbs, flapping our two hands together like a single bird.

The handshake I shared with Sean, my best friend since childhood. The friend who had seen me through thick and thin. Who had carried me whenever I was down. Who, even now, was letting me crash on his couch even though his wife would rather I had left at least a week ago.

Sean had always been my strength, when mine was failing. As I had been for him. So I gave him my muscles.

I was nothing more than skeleton then, but somehow I could feel the flap of Freyja's wings as she bore me to my final trial.

I had no idea where I was. I couldn't see, couldn't hear, couldn't even feel what was under the bones of my feet. So I stood still for a moment, hoping something would happen. That whoever or whatever my final trial was, that it would become somehow clear to me.

But nothing was happening.

I tried to think of who it might be. What I might have left unfinished, or who I might have wronged who had some claim on my bones, on the deepest part of me.

But I could think of nothing. Handing out parts of myself had taken a lot out of me, as it were.

With no good ideas left, I held my bony hands in front of me, and started my jagged, puppetish gait forward.

Stop.

I didn't hear that voice. Not really. Except that I sort of did. The only thing I could think of was that the sound must have been resonating in my bare bones.

Then again, I was in a place where the laws of physics were more like guidelines. So I'm pretty sure any explanation I came up with would have fallen short.

Anyway, I stopped.

I tried to ask who it was stopping me, but I had no voice. Nothing could come out. And thinking the words as loudly as I could didn't seem to do me any good.

So I thought about that voice. One word was all I'd heard, but it seemed to me to have been two tones. Not one deeper than the other, not really, but one ... harsh and the other gentle.

I started forward again, and when the word repeated my bones froze in place.

I'd gotten what I'd wanted though. A chance to hear that voice again. And this time I was sure of it, two tones. One harsh, one gentle. Two tones, one voice. That sounded familiar. Something my grandfather once said...

Hel, goddess of the underworld. Her skin was said to have two tones. Half the pale flesh of a Norse woman, half an icy shade of blue.

That got my bones rattling. Something was wrong. Something had to be wrong. Why had Freyja taken me to Hel? Had I failed? Gotten one of the trials wrong? Instead of rebirth, was I to die?

No. That couldn't be it. Hel, if I was right about her identity, had told me to stop. Which meant I must have been standing on the edge of her realm. Not inside it.

But if I gave her my bones, the last thing I had left, wasn't that the same as dying?

There was no deeper level left of me, and there was no other option I could think of. I stood before Hel herself, and all I had to offer were my bones.

It had all seemed so simple before I started. A new life. A new start. I hadn't thought about the fact in order for a new life to birth, the old life had to cease.

Maybe this was all more literal than I thought. Maybe I wasn't going to get some fresh start as Erik Nilsson, but get born again as a brand new baby. All of the failures I'd had as Erik Nilsson purged from my scorecard, perhaps, but so would be all my future hopes and dreams.

I'd wanted a fresh start, but maybe I hadn't understood just what that entailed...

No.

No. I was not going to die here. No. I was not surrendering myself. Not entirely. I was giving up the life I'd led, not the person I was.

I did it all by act of will then. I offered Hel my bones, not by handing them to her as I'd done with every other offering, but by willing them to be hers while I imagined myself stepping out of my very bones. Shuffling off the very last piece of my mortal coil.

She took my bones, and then I had nothing.

I was free.

THE LIGHTNESS THAT CAME OVER ME THEN WAS DIZZYING. INEBRIATING. I whirled and swirled, though I had no idea where I was or where I was going. It just felt so good to soar. I might have done nothing else until the day of Ragnarök, if not for Freyja.

Freyja must have been watching the entire time. Or maybe she'd simply returned for me in her own time. With even my bones gone, I had no sense of time at all.

All I knew for certain was that I felt the sudden constraints on my movement, and I knew in an instant that once more Freyja's talons had me.

Then I was back in my body. Sort of.

I mean, it was definitely my body, right down to the clothes I was wearing. But instead of sitting on a mountaintop – even a pathetic excuse for a mountaintop – I was standing among lush, green grass at the foot of a great ash tree whose limbs soared off into the sky even as its great roots dug down into the earth.

A huge serpent gnawed at those roots, and a half-dozen harts took one look at me and ran off.

The serpent ignored me, though it didn't ignore the squirrel that came down and chittered at it. The serpent seemed to listen, then hissed at the squirrel, which turned and scrambled back up the trunk.

"Do you know them?" said a woman's voice so sweet it spread from my ears through my body like honey.

I turned, and the woman was as beautiful as her voice. Her hair shimmered in colors from the sheen of pure gold through the brilliance of candle flames. Her face and figure so lovely I fell to my knees, helpless before her. She wore a golden gown, but a brown, feathered cloak.

Freyja.

"I asked if you knew them," she said, her tone one of playful amusement.

I had to shake myself to be able to answer.

"The squirrel. I think his name is Ratatoskr?"

"Yes," she said, "and the serpent is Nídhöggr. You will have to learn these things, you know."

"I will?"

"Of course. I will not have an ignorant *seidhmadhr*."

"*Seidhmadhr*? Me?"

She laughed, and the sound was the childhood joy of opening birthday presents. "You called me in your grandfather's name to remake your life. What did you expect?"

Her laughter trailed away, as did the world around me.

MY EYES BLINKED OPEN. I WAS REALLY BACK IN MY BODY NOW. I KNEW immediately by the roaring complaints of my empty stomach, as well as those of my cramping legs and back, and my sleeping butt. My mouth was dry as the dirt and rocks underneath me.

I was back on the peak of little Mount Dagny, and in the chill morning air I could see the first rays of morning sunlight stream from behind me.

Straightening out my body was not an easy thing. The poor thing had been sitting all night while ... while my soul was traveling between the worlds?

I'd been desperate enough to try it, but I don't know that I'd really believed it would work. Then again, maybe it hadn't. Maybe I'd just dreamed the whole thing.

I hopped up and down on the cold stone rock while my jaw worked and worked at the gritty, vaguely chocolate meal bar that stuck to my teeth and filled my nose with a chemical undersmell that I tried not to think about.

What if it had all been a dream? Was that possible?

I'd been so stressed lately. Pressed to the edge by everything from my collapsing business to the death of my beloved Strider, to Tina's leaving me, to Sean's wife hinting that I had to have family that would take me in.

More out of habit than anything else, I pulled out my cell phone to check my messages. Saw that one of my distributors had called last night, and somehow managed to not wake me up.

I sighed and played the waiting voice message.

"Erik, this in John Grady. Sorry to bother you at this hour, but our quarterly accounting found an error that we missed when reconciling with you. And Erik, I think this one will put a smile on your face. Give me a call first thing in the morning."

I blinked at my phone as I hung up. The last time I'd talked to Grady he'd been calling me "Mr. Nilsson" and sounded like he thought I was cheating him.

But now...

A chill went down my spine that had nothing to do with the early morning air. I'd been ready to write off the whole experience of last night as a dream, but...

I heard the rustle of a falcon's wings, and the distant sound of sweet, honeyed laughter.

SIGN UP FOR STEFON'S NEWSLETTER

Stefon loves to keep in touch with his readers, and loves to keep you reading. The best way for him to do both is for you to sign up for his newsletter.

Sign up at http://www.stefonmears.com/join

If you sign up for Stefon's newsletter, you get...

- Monthly updates about his publishing and travel schedules
- His latest news, in brief, and answers to reader questions
- A free short story for signing up
- List-only offers and occasional specials
- Plus a free short story every month!

ABOUT THE AUTHOR

Stefon Mears knows the sound of Freyja's voice. Stefon has more than thirty books to his credit, and he never stops writing. He earned his M.F.A. in Creative Writing from N.I.L.A., and his B.A. in Religious Studies (double emphasis in Ritual and Mythology) from U.C. Berkeley. He's a lifelong gamer and fantasy fan. Stefon lives in Portland, Oregon, with his wife and three cats.

Look for Stefon online:
www.stefonmears.com
himself@stefonmears.com